HUNTED

OUTRUN. OUTLAST. OUTWIT.

Beyond The Tale

Edited By Briony Kearney

First published in Great Britain in 2020 by:

Young Writers
Remus House
Coltsfoot Drive
Peterborough
PE2 9BF
Telephone: 01733 890066
Website: www.youngwriters.co.uk

Printed and bound in the UK by BookPrintingUK
Website: www.bookprintinguk.com
YB0439K

FOREWORD

IF YOU'VE BEEN SEARCHING FOR EPIC ADVENTURES, TALES OF SUSPENSE AND IMAGINATIVE WRITING THEN SEARCH NO MORE! YOUR HUNT IS AT AN END WITH THIS ANTHOLOGY OF MINI SAGAS.

We challenged secondary school students to craft a story in just 100 words. In this first installment of our SOS Sagas, their mission was to write on the theme of 'Hunted'. But they weren't restricted to just predator vs prey, oh no. They were encouraged to think beyond their first instincts and explore deeper into the theme.

The result is a variety of styles and genres and, as well as some classic cat and mouse games, inside these pages you'll find characters looking for meaning, people running from their darkest fears or maybe even death itself on the hunt.

Here at Young Writers it's our aim to inspire the next generation and instill in them a love for creative writing, and what better way than to see their work in print? The imagination and skill within these pages are proof that we might just be achieving that aim! Well done to each of these fantastic authors.

So if you're ready to find out if the hunter will become the hunted, read on!

CONTENTS

Gabriel Dass (15)	61
Aadam Hussain (14)	62
Saif Samin (11)	63
Harmanjot Singh (12)	64
Lewis Goddard (15)	65
Karisun Pirapaharan (12)	66
Benjamin Kuffa (11)	67
Cameron Lai (12)	68
Roneet Shekhar (12)	69
Ehan Taseen (12)	70
Osman Alqaqaa	71
Abdelrahim (11)	
Arun Jaswal (15)	72
Eisa Ali Yacoob (15)	73
Adam Khalid Khan (14)	74
Manveer Ballagan (11)	75
Abdul Majid (14)	76
Raihan Ali (16)	77
Christopher Lee (16)	78
Harvey Nandra (11)	79
Shiven Singh (11)	80
Nyrun Hargun (16)	81
Armaan Hussain (14)	82
Taha Umar (11)	83
Arjun Sohanpal (11)	84
Pravit Vashisht (11)	85
Eran Luyima (11)	86
Hardev Manku (12)	87
Muhammed Nasim Ahmed	88
Tinron Chan (11)	89
Raahil Junaid (14)	90
Jay Gaddu (11)	91
Mustapha Haris (14)	92
Muhammad Moosa Raza (11)	93
Zayan Arshad (12)	94
Hamza Arif (12)	95
Anthony Simon Maczka (15)	96
Amaan Siddique (15)	97
Ahmed Osman (11)	98
Callum Mann (11)	99
Ismaeel Ali (11)	100
Abdul Rehman (11)	101
Arjun Lyall (12)	102

Chetan Dhami (12)	103
John Obayelu (11)	104
Mohammad Bilal Ahmad (16)	105
Oliver Fance (12)	106
Muhammad Amir Zaier (16)	107
Erjon Beqiri (11)	108
Ajay Phull (11)	109
Arjun Kalirai (15)	110
Abdullah Faisal Jamil (11)	111
Jashandeep Singh (11)	112
Hamthan Farish (12)	113
Yousuf Assaf Bashir (11)	114
Rayaan Iqbal (12)	115
Diego Kerr (11)	116
Ahmed Patel (15)	117
Aryan Singh Kular (11)	118
Jai Whitehouse (12)	119
Rafiad Choudhury (12)	120
Michael Matthew White (11)	121
Ibaad Qureshi (11)	122
Joshan Kudhail (12)	123
Max Ho (12)	124
Amin Mohammad Khakssar (11)	125
Yusef Hakim (12)	126
Mohammad Shayan (11)	127
Neil Chen (16)	128
Ritish Sadhra (16)	129
Zakariya Nawaz (11)	130
Osman Yahia (11)	131

The Wigston Academies Trust, Wigston

Oliver Bailey (13)	132
Merlin Otto Lee (12)	133
Sukhman Bajwa (12)	134
Riley Grycuk (12)	135
Cameron Lee (13)	136
Kane Munday (13)	137
Alyssa Eve Vaja (13)	138
Isabelle Tait (13)	139
Rhys Holyland (11)	140
Bethany Fothergill (16)	141
Luca Franco Moroni (13)	142

Ruby Heathcote (12)	143	Iain Weatherby (14)	183
Chi La (12)	144	J Hynd (13)	184
Holly Derbyshire (13)	145	Shanice W	185
Molly Hanney (13) & Marissa	146	Hana Toulson (14)	186
Faye McFarlane (12)		Kane Hampson (14)	187
Natasha Taylor (13)	147	Dawn Dyson (13)	188
Hannah Bigden (11)	148	Molly McSweeney (14)	189
Matty Dolan (11)	149	Elise Jennifer Erin Hustings (13)	190
Raegan Erin Hamp (13)	150	Ashley Jones (13)	191
Owen Lunn (11)	151	Zack James Bingham (12)	192
Paige Sherwin (13)	152	Kieran T	193
Hannah Vann (13)	153	Jude Chambers (12)	194
Harry Wells (11)	154	Seth Wright	195
Maisie Keane (13)	155	Ashleigh Tinsley	196
Freya Mistry (13)	156	Thomas Oxley (12)	197
Macauli Moran (13)	157	Arran Gray (13)	198
Macey Jane Liquorish (13)	158	Reece Bowling (13)	199
Ruby Kendall (11)	159	Maddison Parfitt	200
Marissa Faye McFarlane (12)	160	Mason Gardner (13)	201
Tia Hill (11)	161	Maddison R	202
Jack Smart (12)	162	Matthew Meadows (12)	203
Woody Orton (13)	163	Amelia Finch (12)	204
Lili Rutter (12)	164	Toms Trahovcevs	205
Frances Mitchell (12)	165	Keira H (14)	206
Milly Jade Shaw (12)	166	Ben Harwood (12)	207
Sara Filali (12)	167		
Grace Sheffield (11)	168		
Eleanor Reece-Sumner (12)	169		
Louis Cockshaw (12)	170		
Emma-Louise Little (12)	171		
Martin John Bourne-Fisher (12)	172		
Isobel Henderson (11)	173		

Wellfield High School, Leyland

Morgan Ellen Armer (14)	174
Leon Whatton (15)	175
Ellie D	176
Pearl Xu (14)	177
Maddy O'Neill	178
Abby Bamford (12)	179
Bethany Moulding (13)	180
Amy Smith (12)	181
Maddie Wilson-Burgess	182

THE STORIES

The Attacker

"Don't go into the woods," they told me. Doesn't mean I would listen to them...

I quickened my pace, running away from the attacker. Who would want to hurt me? My feet ached from the distance, making the reality of being caught sink in. I needed to know who would want me dead. My legs gave in under me and I fell to the ground, with my attacker approaching closer and closer. The dark figure removed its hood, revealing my younger sister, knife in hand.

"Why, Katie?"

"You were always their favourite."

Darkness took me, slowly leaving life behind me...

Aminat Oreoluwa Sholanke (12)

Fort Pitt Grammar School, Chatham

The Hunt Of Truths

"We have to leave. Now!"

The sirens screamed, blocking the sound of our heavy heartbeats. The ground became jelly as we ran deeper into the bleak night. The surroundings soon became a blur. Footsteps. Closer, nearer.

"They're closing in!"

Trees loomed over like skyscrapers, their bare branches fingers ready to grab at us at any second. *Bang!* It was over. It all happened so fast. We were chained up like animals and taken away. We didn't mean to do it. If only they understood, but who would believe us? They found out and now we had to pay the price.

Katie Smart (13)
Fort Pitt Grammar School, Chatham

The Chase

They knew. What could I do now? I heard sirens coming towards me. Panic-struck, I ran. No intentions, nothing. The sirens were becoming clearer in the distance. Panicking more, I ran faster than I thought I could. The sirens slowly started to fade in the background until I heard some coming around the corner. There was nothing I could do except run. I turned around, trying to run in the opposite direction, hoping they wouldn't catch me. But the sirens got louder and I was starting to lose my energy. As they got louder, I got slower. Oh no...

Mackenzie Collins (12)
Fort Pitt Grammar School, Chatham

Claws

We had to leave. Now. She dragged me from the floor, a puddle of thick blood remained where it left me to die. Red oozed from my wrist, trickling down my scuffed arm. Images of its distorted, unsightly face flashed through my mind. Its incisive claws ripping into my arm and scarred my thoughts. If this mysterious girl hadn't come to rescue me, I'd surely be dead by now. But then her eyes widened and she let out an ear-piercing scream, staring at something behind me. That's when I felt the same knife-like claws closing around my neck.

Laura Pearson (15)
Fort Pitt Grammar School, Chatham

The Stalker

He was standing there. Again. All dressed in darkest black. My heart rate increased as quick as lightning. I tried to walk away but couldn't, my legs wouldn't let me move. Then before I realised what was happening, he was bolting towards me.

I screamed and ran, my dress sticking to my back. His legs were much longer than mine, so he caught up with me quite quickly. I darted into a dark alleyway, slipping and sliding in the mud. The gate at the end was locked. The man gripped my hand. A note: 'You have twenty-four hours...'

Elena Amobi (11)
Fort Pitt Grammar School, Chatham

Knock, Knock

We had to leave. Now. At least, that's what he told me. A zombie apocalypse, there was no other way to explain it. The weeping murmurs and the vigorous banging on my back door. It was just us, everyone else wasn't human. They continued trying to break in. He was all I had. He pushed himself forcefully against the back door. The banging grew deafening, ringing in my ears. My palms sweating, I could hear my heart in my ears. I sprinted upstairs. The banging stopped yet the floorboards were creaking. I heard a scream. I should've listened to him.

Sydney Budenbender (13)
Fort Pitt Grammar School, Chatham

Nothing Hurts

We were close. It hurt. Blinking my eyes open, the darkness swallowed me up. The cold breached my skin, chilling me to the bone. Now was not the time to think, just act. Dead or alive, six feet under, on the surface, what's the difference? Pounding in my ears, was it the approaching footsteps or my racing heart? I crouched down, my legs numb from running. I threaded my dirty fingers through my shrivelled hair. I was short on air, gagging continuously. I dropped onto my side. It all fell still and silent. It didn't hurt anymore Nothing did now.

Rebecca Moldoveanu (12)
Fort Pitt Grammar School, Chatham

Ready Or Not, Here I Come

My childhood all over again: worse. A small, little game of hide-and-seek, they said. But thirty-four people had already been captured. Who knew where?

I was alone, behind a small bin in a dark alleyway. In the distance were several screams of agony. Suddenly, footsteps. I saw a large shadow slowly emerge from the corner.

"Ready or not, here I come," it muttered.

My heart raced and my hands shook. Oh no - I had an itch. Surely if I moved a tiny bit, they wouldn't hear? Oops. It wasn't safe any longer.

Isabel Bedford (12)
Fort Pitt Grammar School, Chatham

Twenty-Four Hours On The Run

I had twenty-four hours... The hunt was on. I ran, following with every step like theirs. It was hard but possible. They disappeared. I stared, I looked everywhere but all I could see was doors. They were all surrounding me. Where would they take me? I decided not to go in them and turn back. But if I turned back, then the twenty-four hours would be over. I looked at every door closely. They had numbers, which one should I go in? One, two, three...? I didn't know! The twenty-four hours was almost over. I checked, the time had gone.

Maya Pillai-Hill (11)
Fort Pitt Grammar School, Chatham

The Hunters

I had an hour left to complete the challenge, if I didn't I would be thrown into a cage and dumped into the middle of the ocean with a blindfold on. I had three keys left to find, all locked in boxes dotted around the terrace. I started to hyperventilate. As my vision became blurry, I wanted to scream help but nothing came out. The hunters were banging on the door, rattling the doorknob, trying to attack. I lost my consciousness as they heaved their way in. They threw me into the cage... That was it. I was done for.

Eleanor Rose (12)
Fort Pitt Grammar School, Chatham

Twenty-Four Hours

I had twenty-four hours to live. Sirens were screeching in my ear and the predators were on the loose. It was pitch-black. Many thoughts were racing through my mind. I was lost. Screams echoing in the gloomy black hole. As I walked closer to the screams, I saw blood splattered across the walls and the floor. Someone or something was there and it had taken the soul of the unlucky victim. I began to hear footsteps. I ran and I ran but it was too late. It found me. Its horrid growl came closer. The predator had found its prey!

Jessica Wright (12)

Fort Pitt Grammar School, Chatham

The Clear Blue Sea

The radiating sun danced on the clear, blue waves as I surfed peacefully. Suddenly, the sun was enclosed by a dark, miserable cloud. A violent wave crashed down on me, thrusting me into the depths of the sea. My eyes stung. My throat dry, my lungs empty. I threw my exhausted body frantically around, trying to catch a breath. It was pointless. I caught a glimpse of a shadow creeping on the sea bed. My eyes gazed up to see a grey, gilled monster speeding towards me. His beady eyes fixed on me. I was being hunted. I was prey.

Isabella Seare (11)

Fort Pitt Grammar School, Chatham

The End

We were close but not close enough. I watched as everyone sprinted ahead. I was on my own. The forest was gloomy and cold. I knew they were close, watching. Slowly, very slowly, I made my way closer and closer to the end. But this was just the beginning. I knew at some point that I'd be taking my last breath. The trees were whispering, it felt as though they knew something I didn't. Consequently, the world closed in on me and I knew it was over. Then, there they were. Smug was written all over their rotten, filthy faces...

Molly Priddle (12)
Fort Pitt Grammar School, Chatham

The Sea

As day collapsed into night, my life became suffocated. Sirens blared; the chase was on. I wished the night would devour me. With the sea in front of me, slapping the shore, I knew what I had to do: swim. Sirens engulfed me, my heart hammered against my chest. Thoughts bombarded me. *Splash!* Crisp water absorbed me and blackness destroyed everything in my line of view. Even though I felt like I had been sucked into a black hole, I kept on swimming. Within the water, a sense of safety blanketed me. Or so I thought!

Emily Teeton (11)
Fort Pitt Grammar School, Chatham

No Escape

The sound of creaking floorboards echoed above me. A huge wave of panic crashed over my body. I'd been locked up inside this hellhole for what seemed an eternity, with no escape. Every time I got a chance to explore for an exit, all possibilities were locked. If there was a way to freedom, I could never defeat the wrath of... it. The creaking came to a halt, now was the time to move. My life depended on it. I took the risk and ran, but was soon followed by the daunting footsteps of the predator. It was hunting me.

Sophie Nicole Brookwell (13)

Fort Pitt Grammar School, Chatham

The Virus Of Techtown

Ricky and her friend Edward were working in a top-secret lab for children who had graduated early. They worked day and night, working on computer software for the mayor. They were so tired of working day and night, that they created a virus. Instead, the virus spread worldwide, it took over all computers. So they ran fast, with twenty-four hours to live. They thought they were being tracked down. That was why the policemen were following them. So they hid in a cave, it was pitch-black. They were shivering and scared.

Amaoge Okoli (11)
Fort Pitt Grammar School, Chatham

3, 2, 1... Run!

It was a dark, dreary night. I stood upon the moonlit sky in the isolated forest. I could see light, but not the light I thought - they were coming for me.

I hurtled out of my tent. I ran as fast as I could but they were getting closer. My heart was racing, I thought it was going to explode out of my chest. I kept running, faster and faster, longing for hope.

Each step burnt my chest but I knew I had to keep running. I found myself in the road, headlights heading towards me. "It's coming!" *Bang!*

Morgana Davison (11)
Fort Pitt Grammar School, Chatham

Hunter To Hunted

It was that night I got the dreaded phone call. I never thought I would end up being the one who had to pay. You're probably wondering what I'm talking about. Well, let me explain...

I was the person who was hunting. In helicopters, searching for the desired villain. We were high in the sky above the masking woods. Just then, it all switched. What did I hear? I was the hunted. Wow, didn't see that coming. Yep, a sly old fox framed me. My time was up. The tables had turned. And I had something to say about it.

Orla Murphy (11)
Fort Pitt Grammar School, Chatham

War

Just keep running. It's close. How much longer have I got? My lifeless legs burn in pain. Screaming and gasping, I know this is the end. I feel it deep down in my weary bones. I have to keep going. I can't stop now. The deafening rumble of machine guns piercing my ears. Tears streaming down my face, I thrust my gas mask on and savour the last oxygen I can steal. "Gas!" I scream, with all I have left. Like a yellow beast, it hunts me down. I crouch down as it swallows me. Darkness. Gone forever.

Charlotte Crampton (12)
Fort Pitt Grammar School, Chatham

Werewolf!

We were close, I knew it. I smelt the faint smell of blood that made me sick. Night had come, time to transform. This bullet was going in their foul, revolting bodies. I was finally going to have their heads hung up on my wall. I obtained my rifle and set off into the brutal forest that longed to rip me apart. I heard murmurs, then I knew I was close. After following the way of the winding and perplexing twists and turns, and vicious cuts and bruises, after all that, I was not ready for what I saw... werewolf!

Ayomi Eugenia Ojo (11)
Fort Pitt Grammar School, Chatham

Ex

I couldn't run for much longer. My heart pounding, feeling sick with worry. Rain spat from the sky, it obscured my vision. Stumbling along through crooked trees, a knife came shooting at me, lodging into my leg. I turned, he was there. I thought he loved me. What did I do? Blood flooded out of my leg, leaving a trail. I stumbled over a rock, going unconscious. I woke up with him leaning over me, he held the knife to my neck. I kicked him off, got up and ran as fast as I could. I wouldn't ever be safe.

Eve Florence Wyatt (12)
Fort Pitt Grammar School, Chatham

Framed

Isolated in a sea of faces, they studied my every move. Each accusation echoed in my mind, yet I couldn't make out what they were saying. My heart pounded in my ears as I swallowed back my tears and screamed at the top of my lungs in agony. A frosty silence dusted the atmosphere - I could feel every single pair of eyes tearing into me. Suddenly, the crowd advanced, nearing closer with each second. Without hesitation, I sprinted away, faster than ever. Until all the voices were only whispers between the trees.

Erin McIntyre (12)
Fort Pitt Grammar School, Chatham

Hunted

Her blonde ponytail swished when she bounced on the sidewalk. Out of the blue, the bright flashes of lightning lit up the dark sky. She picked up her pace when a car came silently down the road. It pulled over and a man got out. He made his way over to her. The girl, oblivious to him, carried on. The man swiftly drew out his glistening knife and skillfully jabbed it into her back.

I screamed. The man looked at me and began to hurry over. I ran. One thing was for sure, he wouldn't give up. I was hunted.

Annabelle Head (12)

Fort Pitt Grammar School, Chatham

The Forest Run

It was a gloomy and frightening night, the trees towered over me as if they were putting me in a deathtrap. I knew it wasn't long until the sirens would start whining, so I decided to start finding a place that was safe.

It was getting darker and my legs painfully ached. Every place I ran to looked the same. I ran further. I could barely breathe, while sweat was pouring down my face. I closed my eyes and my heart skipped a beat as I heard the ear-bleeding ring of the sirens. I was being hunted...

Amelia Togneri (11)
Fort Pitt Grammar School, Chatham

Criminal Minds

The sky was pitch-black and I could still hear their footsteps getting nearer by the second. I had to keep running but my heart was pumping, I had to stop.

At last, I crept down an alleyway on the side of the road, the moon glistening onto my pale face. The air smelled dry and the ground was made of red brick. As I desperately tried to regain my breath, my ears pricked up. I heard them and, soon enough, they turned the corner. My whole body tensed as I wondered, *will I get out of here alive?*

Georgia Pendleton (13)

Fort Pitt Grammar School, Chatham

It Starts Now

I had twenty-four hours but, until the sirens wailed, the hunt was not on. Red and blue vividly flashing in my eyes, I waited, with sweat running down my face. The monotoned sirens went, the sound travelling far and wide. I was being hunted. I ran, I ran as fast as I could. There was nowhere to hide, no one to run to. Voices in my head, sirens still haunting my ears, I continued running, hoping to find someone or somewhere to hide. I ran until my legs could take no more. Footsteps... I was being hunted.

Leila Phillips (11)

Fort Pitt Grammar School, Chatham

The Chase

We have to leave. Now. The freed experiments and I have made it past the guards but we aren't safe yet. We may have got out of the government facility but nowhere is safe in this country. Suddenly, growls pierce the icy air. The trained have been released - our nightmare is now our reality. Our legs move faster as our panic grows. This is the one chance to get out of that godforsaken place. We all know that as soon as we cross that border there is no going back. We will be hunted by the world forever...

Eleanor Scruton (12)

Fort Pitt Grammar School, Chatham

Eyes

I had to leave! I felt a cold tingle on the hairs of my back; I saw, in the dark, dilated pupils glaring at me as I stood there shivering, paralysed. I glanced around me, looking for an appropriate tree to climb - taking my eyes off the beast for a second. When I looked back, it was gone. I felt the same tingly feeling on my back. Then everything went black. I woke up; I couldn't move. My body was bruised and I was tied down with metal chains. I struggled and felt a piercing pain across my skull.

Amber Ward (12)
Fort Pitt Grammar School, Chatham

Trapped

My feet pound the earth, leaves scatter in my wake. I hear more feet behind me but I don't dare look back. I hurdle a fence and suddenly I'm in a garden. I scramble desperately for a way out. I exhale, the gate is unlocked. Infinitely tall buildings surround me and the fumes smack me in the face. Warm air rushes through my cropped hair. I spot a back-alley through the corner of my eye and dart in. It's a dead-end. My chest tightens, I hear them coming. Closer. Closer. I'm trapped.

Jemima Judd
Fort Pitt Grammar School, Chatham

Hunted By Fear

As I sat on the plane, grasping the armrests, I felt like I was being drowned in my own ocean of fear; like my bubble of safety had burst from the pressure of the anxiety I was feeling. Planes were my worst nightmare - anything could happen, with no way out. The seat belt light had come on. Time to take off. I tried to swallow the lump of fear rising in my throat. It was taking over my body, beating my lungs until I couldn't breathe. I was telling myself it'd be fine, but I was hunted by my own fear.

Jasmine Trevena (13)
Fort Pitt Grammar School, Chatham

Keep Running

I could feel the adrenaline running through my bones. I knew telling them was a risk but I couldn't hold it in for much longer. It was wrong! He insisted we keep running, not to dare stop. We were out of breath and rested for a few seconds. He spotted something - a car. The keys were under the tyre. At this point, I was terrified. He told me to get in, that he could do it. We drove for a while, until his eyes started to droop. I suggested we stop, I told him we didn't have to do this.

Peniel Agaga (13)
Fort Pitt Grammar School, Chatham

The Ravenclaw Sequel

She would be dead soon. I had to find her. One dying wish; one last hope. Where was she? The anticipation was destroying me. The forests of Albania, she had to be there. I fumbled through the trees, the darkness obscuring my vision. Then I saw it. A wisp of golden hair. I skidded to a halt in front of her. I pleaded with her but she refused to return. My anger rose to the point of death. I plunged my dagger into her. What had I done? Regret flooded me. I had to do it. I mirrored her death.

Violet Grace Pond (12)
Fort Pitt Grammar School, Chatham

The Wolf Hunt

I was close. The trees around me were swaying from side to side, whistling in the wind. The moon shone bright in the sky. I heard a howl, they were coming.

I tried to pull my legs out of the snow, my toes were frozen. I knew I didn't have much time. More howls came from the top of the mountain. They were coming.

Lightning struck the ground and sent a shiver down my spine. I pinched myself to make sure I wasn't dreaming. I could hear them getting closer. This was the end.

Abby Theobald (13)

Fort Pitt Grammar School, Chatham

The Chase

The sirens shrieked; the hunt was on. My heart was in my mouth. All I could hear was my heart pounding. I smelt the fresh dampness of the autumn leaves. I could feel the eyes of bloodthirsty predators lurking over me. A twig snapped. My head spun. I ran. I didn't stop until sunrise. As I ran, the trees passed by me faster and faster until the woods came to an end. I stood, staring out at a desolate wasteland. I turned around. There they were, staring at me. Ready to kill.

Emily Carrick (11)
Fort Pitt Grammar School, Chatham

Hunted

I couldn't run for much longer. My legs were in pain. My heart was about to pop out of my chest. I could hear the sirens getting louder. My head felt heavy and then, darkness. I heard gunshots, I heard shouting. My eyes peeled open, my hand in a pool of blood. I saw my mum. Crying, she was. I dragged my mum into the jaws of death. I tried to get up and run but I was tied down. Before I knew it, my mum was dead. Shot between the eyes. Dead on the floor. "Help," I screeched.

Abigail Garthwaite (13)

Fort Pitt Grammar School, Chatham

Ready Or Not, Here I Come

My legs felt like jelly. I wanted to just roll into a ball, scream and shriek - but I couldn't. It was all his fault, if he hadn't been so greedy, if he hadn't chased this desire so deeply, they wouldn't have found us. It was like a game of hide-and-seek, the only difference was the ending. I scanned the area around me, it was like a blanket of darkness. Then the outline of a human appeared with a look and thirst for revenge. I'm supposed to be the hunter, not the hunted!

Yana Jones (12)
Fort Pitt Grammar School, Chatham

Escape

As I run, they follow behind me with their screeching sirens and bright, vivid colours calling out to me. I turn the corner and try to lose them. It doesn't work. They accelerate! This is it. They're going to trap me! It's a dead-end! The cars come to a halt. Left or right? Prison or freedom? I only have moments to escape. What am I going to do? They jump out of the cars. They are close, closer than anyone has been before. They stand, staring at me...

Elizabeth Grace Rye (11)
Fort Pitt Grammar School, Chatham

Death Is Near

I haven't eaten since my brother died in the war. He was sixteen when he passed away. But even now, six months on, I can still see his body lying motionless on the battlefield. Dead. But whoever killed him is about to kill me. I have anorexia, an eating disorder. I have starved myself for the last six months and it is a miracle that I am still alive so I won't be able to run. I only have a few weeks to live, so I guess I will see you in Heaven, my little brother.

Isabella Marroquin (12)
Fort Pitt Grammar School, Chatham

Arrows

The leaves rustling, my breath disappearing as I dodge the deadly arrows, I hear a stick snap next to me. Out comes another arrow. I stop. I panic, then I duck. They are coming from every side. I am trapped. As I howl, the pack come and make them trapped. Then they turn their backs to me, so I attack them. I don't accept their apologies. They are soon dead. Look who's the hunter now.

Libby Sherwood (12)
Fort Pitt Grammar School, Chatham

Prison Break

The sirens wailed, off I went. Running for miles and miles, desperate to catch my breath. Shouts, cheering and alarms were all I heard until I was out.

I continued to run until an open car was in sight. I hopped in the car and drove as fast as I could. A police car soon crashed into me. I was unconscious.

It was pitch-black as I awoke. There I was, in a cell. It was over.

Hannah Rose Pearce (13)
Fort Pitt Grammar School, Chatham

Escaped

Sirens were wailing, people were fleeing and Area 51 was in chaos! In the distance, something was moving; something grotesque, something not human. Flashes of green flew past. The abomination was escaping into the forest and nothing could stop it. A soldier fired wildly; a stray bullet pierced into its racing heart but nothing happened... if anything, it angered it! It let out an earth-trembling roar and the forest caught fire. Some people were running, some people were standing still, perplexed by what they had just witnessed. But one thing was certain: there was no stopping the crusading monster...

Adam Crawford (11)
Hutton CE Grammar School, Hutton

Abandoned

My heart vigorously pounded at my chest. My legs uncontrollably trembled as I hid around the corner. Fortunately, 'it' didn't notice me turn the corner.

As soon as I lost sight of 'it', I felt something touch my shoulder. In fright, I jolted myself away and suddenly began to run.

"Don't worry, it's me, Malcolm." Instantaneously, my body stopped. It was my best friend, Malcolm. "Let's go home," said Malcolm.

Boom! The loud sound of a gunshot pierced my ears.

"Aah!" cried Malcolm, in agony.

'It' was back; 'it' wasn't going to stop until blood dripped from my body...

Adrian Nyamongo (16)
King Edward VI Handsworth Grammar School For Boys, Handsworth

Sentimental

I could faintly hear the sound of guards panicking over the ear-splitting alarms. "December has escaped!"
"Damn right," I hissed to myself. My head throbbing and legs trembling.
After sixteen years in this nightmare, I'd memorised every corridor, every inch, every step it took for each guard to get out of this hell-hole. The memory of it all kept replaying in my head.
Picking the cell lock was child's play. Next was luring the guards in with a couple of 'dead bodies'. The alarm stopped. "Then they're all in." The gate opened. "And I'm free."

Omar Amin Whaind (15)
King Edward VI Handsworth Grammar School For Boys, Handsworth

Submerged

I stripped myself of the orange jumpsuit labelled '3271'.
Capturing every breath possible, I submerged underneath
the water. My heart dropped, my legs relaxed.
I couldn't see much through the goggles but I had to plough
through. This had never been done before, escaping
Alcatraz. It was said to be impossible. However, there's a
first time for everything.
A bright light glimmered through the glass of my goggles,
rotating from left to right from a distance; it was attached
to a ship-like object. It wasn't the police, as they helped me
with this operation. But it could be *them*...

Junaid Rehman (16)
King Edward VI Handsworth Grammar School For Boys, Handsworth

Illusions And Delusions

Scolded and injured, I couldn't run from it any longer. The mistake had been made and there was nothing I could do to countermand it. Debilitated and fatigued, I didn't know what to do... but run.

The Devil's necromancy was working; every inhalation turned into needles, injecting anaesthesia into my veins, shielding me from the torment. The archaic being had now been awakened from the abyss of wickedness.

Sharply, hollow craters opened up beneath me as I howled for mercy. A ghastly grin wrinkled its lips as it gazed upon me. Uttering maledictions, the seance slowly morphed into a trance...

Navtaran Singh Sian (15)
King Edward VI Handsworth Grammar School For Boys, Handsworth

The Facility

The group of friends scattered around, thinking about what to do. The demonic creature was behind them.

"It was here, I swear," whispered Mike.

"Where did you last see it?" stuttered Lucas.

"The last time the gates opened to here, it must've changed," Mike replied.

The group split up to divert the unknown figure. The rooms went black. Max was outrunning the figure until she tripped and fell. The human-like creature wasn't far behind her. *Crash!*

She was in a lot of trouble. Max was tired and everyone else had hidden away. The figure dropped, but something worse appeared.

Taran Patel (12)
King Edward VI Handsworth Grammar School For Boys, Handsworth

Lost In Translation

The fog slept on the wing above the drowned camp where the last glimmering lamps made slumber. The sound of graphite dancing across scraps of decaying newspapers echoed along the wind.

Chaya, though quite young, couldn't cope with her senile complexion - risking her life every day. Instead, she relied on her artistic talents to liberate her true beauty. The gloomy camp uninhabited, for all but Chaya were hidden under the shadows. The moon illuminated her. The fog lifted. A figure, tall, broad, closed in on her. His rifle resting in his holster. His rough hand caressing her flushed cheek...

Dharam Rana (15)
King Edward VI Handsworth Grammar School For Boys, Handsworth

Beautiful Nature

Rain didn't fall but was driven, merciless and torrential. The trees didn't sway but bent and groaned whilst their limbs were torn apart. The gale-force wind brushed past nature and thrust the autumn leaves, not like confetti but like the devil's ammunition.

But I needed a place to hide; I was determined. Thrusting my body, I arrived at a church. Desperately, I tugged at the gate. Under the fog, disgusting pity suppressed my desperation.

The pandemonium as the storm encircled me, haunting me. Then, suddenly, the cacophonous roar fell. Simple sincerity surrounded me. Silence.

Rohan Bagga (14)

King Edward VI Handsworth Grammar School For Boys, Handsworth

Null Sector

They were here. Null Sector had just arrived in London. The ringleader - Bastion was chasing him. Lucio ran across Junkertown, gliding with his skates. Bastion was catching up, he was flying at the literal speed of light towards Lucio. Lucio ran and ran, heart pounding, energy-draining. Bastion's gunshots flying centimetres away from Lucio's face. Lucio was close, he could see the ship from his position. A missile zoomed past his face, blowing the ship out of existence. He was stuck now. He was a goner. He panicked, still running, Bastion's shots all missing him. Suddenly, gunshot. Silence.

Rhuben Mistry-Bhogal (11)
King Edward VI Handsworth Grammar School For Boys, Handsworth

Psychology Of A Businessman

I walked at the same pace as my bleeding heartbeat - a worrying intention.

It seemed nobody wanted to question the congested crimson dribbling along my neck, dyeing my collar a bright pink from an innocent white shirt. Even my smeared Oxfords showed nothing suggesting sanity; this black mirror showed the blurred lines of a deranged businessman. Albeit, I viewed my filtered surroundings in a cursed burgundy. Readying my pace as I readied my blade, I stalked forward with a hushed unnoticeable tone. I could hear her breathing, the same way a prey does when hiding from their predator...

Krishan Patel (15)

King Edward VI Handsworth Grammar School For Boys, Handsworth

The Invasion Of The Memes

We were close until it happened. Our nemeses, Big Chungus, Howard the alien and Thanos ruled the entire universe within minutes. They released their troopers, called 'memes', and the adrenaline inside my body intensified. Pewdiepie and I used a technique called 'Naruto running' into their kingdom, Area 51.

I arrived at the base, a possessed Mike Wazowski and Expand Dong stood in front of us. I gaped in shock.

"Come on! Let's use the power of the bro-fist," Pewdiepie said.

Plenty of their troopers surrounded us, I knew I was in trouble. I stood still in shock and confusion.

Lance Miguel (11)
King Edward VI Handsworth Grammar School For Boys, Handsworth

The Heist

I was fleeing expeditiously from the forsaken facility. I had twenty-four hours to get to the location before they detected that I was missing. My legs were fatigued, my stomach throbbed, my heart was pounding rapidly.
After a few hours, I found a neglected bicycle. I picked it up and drifted to the mysterious location. *Bang!* I heard a gunshot, could it be? Were they now terrorising the city? Every shot was like a volcanic eruption. All I heard were cacophonous explosions. *Boom!* Blood sprinted out of me. My mind went vacant... Was this the end of my dreadful life?

Abdulrahman Hajer (11)

King Edward VI Handsworth Grammar School For Boys, Handsworth

Deadly Nature

Hurtling down the hillside, I hear all my broken bones as they bellow in a shriek of audible pain. Heading face-first towards the pearlescent, inky lake, knowing the water would be like concrete... I turn, staring possessively, watching him as he gets smaller. The last few glimpses of his pale face as a dark 'O' covers his mouth as he screams. He hits the water and almost immediately ricochets off, spinning furiously. He must be dead. Please let it have killed him! However, my focus soon changes, as I too face the plunging abyss. Staring helplessly at my own certain fate.

Mustafaa Ahmed (16)
King Edward VI Handsworth Grammar School For Boys, Handsworth

The Escapees Of The Martian Hunters

Twenty-four hours left to survive. I don't want to leave. I don't want to depart from my family. They're coming to kill and won't stop until they hunt me down.

It's not safe anymore. If they find me, if they recognise me, then I will be dead. There's no time left, they're coming. They're coming to kill.

Because they're coming, I run carelessly to the exit. What have I done? Why are the Martian Hunters after me? I see them out of the corner of my eye. They're looking everywhere. They spot me. They've found me. "Gotcha."

Farhan Hussain (11)

King Edward VI Handsworth Grammar School For Boys, Handsworth

Life To Death

I had fifteen minutes to hide or to die. The jet-black colour of death haunted me, screams of innocence banging in my eardrum, longing to get out. The dark red pool of memories dispersed across the rough city grounds.

There was nowhere to hide. Buildings as straight as soldiers stood alone. Lonely. Corruption and hate reflected upon the moonlit sky. Bullets scattered, lifeless bodies abandoned. Heartless demons with a purpose to ruin humanity.

An assault rifle was pushed into my head. A bullet zoomed through my skull. I saw a light illuminating this once lively, bright world.

Ahmed Asif (11)

King Edward VI Handsworth Grammar School For Boys, Handsworth

The It

It's not safe now they know. They saw the photograph. They'll be coming for me soon.

I have to evacuate the house within one hour and leave 'it' behind.

But I can't leave 'it'. 'It' is the only hope I have. They threatened what they'll do to me if I don't obey them. But now I have a plan.

They don't suspect me of knowing it's power and I *will* use 'it' against them. When they come for 'it', they'll have a surprise.

Suddenly, I'm hit in the head from behind.

"We've got you now. You have no escape."

Dawud Khan (12)
King Edward VI Handsworth Grammar School For Boys, Handsworth

Blood-Soaked Plains

Blood oozed out of the lacerations within my tepid flesh as I stumbled across the desert plains, away from the monstrosity. Roars echoed from the beast, petrified me, bombarded my delicate eardrums. My crimson blood deluged the deserted plains.

Out of pain, my feeble body tumbled. I had no control over the four, slender legs of mine. My heart throbbed as the merciless brute scampered within my radar. *Bang!*

All movement had ceased. I began to see two fly-infested carcasses from above. Slowly, they depreciated in size. I realised my soul had left its abode.

Safwaan Raqeeb (16)
King Edward VI Handsworth Grammar School For Boys, Handsworth

Cell Exposure

When will they stop? They don't need me that badly. The forest's darkness towers over me, making me feel frightened and cold. *Nee-naw!* They've caught up. I needed to escape from the confined space of my cell. Muddy as it is, I carried on, panting with all my power. Each breath is like injecting poison into my organs. Finally, a hole to transform in. I leap into the hole, knowing that they are only a few minutes away. Letting my secret unveil, hands become paws, body becomes hairier, teeth become fangs. The hunters are now the hunted. Something has appeared.

Dhruv Singh-Chowan (11)
King Edward VI Handsworth Grammar School For Boys, Handsworth

The Danger Hunt!

His teeth chattered, his heart pounded like a bass drum, his thoughts raced through his mind. Was he going to die? Was this the end? He knew there was only one thing this implied: he was being hunted!

As he ran, frantically, he noticed he was entering the dark, gloomy woods. Engulfed by trees, more frightened than a rabbit fleeing a fox, he pounced into the miserable, cramped atmosphere. Now he was safe. Well, that's what he thought. The dangerous killing machine grazed through the trees as if they were foam. Surely, this was definitely the end. Or was it?

Daniel Mutekedza (11)
King Edward VI Handsworth Grammar School For Boys, Handsworth

Escape

Thunder snapped and lightning countered while rain ran. Trunks, branches, roots, what wasn't in his way? Finally able to escape the jaws of those hellions, he was now in combat with the forest - of which, nature seemed to back. Regardless, he powered through. Having got this far, he was going all the way. Sounds of distorted barks and crashing paws filled his ears. Hounds had been released. If they caught him, all his efforts were void. He wasn't going to let that happen. The forest finally ended but now a deep, dark, abyssal gap stood. Hope was crushed by despair.

Abdu Miah (15)

King Edward VI Handsworth Grammar School For Boys, Handsworth

Them

Always anxious, it felt as if I was being stalked by them. Perhaps it was nothing, but it felt like they were everywhere. As the cog-wheels clawed their way up the incline, I observed the jagged mountain. In the distance, in the face of the sheer cliff, the stone monastery seemed to hang. From the train to the mountaintop, I saw a solitary figure walking on the platform. The skeleton-like man was draped in the traditional Catholic purple robe. I turned swiftly to inspect my surroundings, I saw another. Both had bony features. Abruptly, I felt a surge of adrenaline.

Gabriel Dass (15)

King Edward VI Handsworth Grammar School For Boys, Handsworth

When Can I Stop?

As soon as three struck, my eyes shot open to the nearby cry of my mother.

"Benjamin!" she shrieked.

I leapt out of my bed, frantically snapping my eyes around the room in utter confusion. The sound of instructions bellowing through my measly body helped me realise what I must do: run.

I squeezed through the tattered window and landed like a frog. Across the road was David, my best friend, stacked on top of his family with his eyes wide open and staring at the sky, where many stars sat. I was clustered with thoughts and, inevitably, I ran.

Aadam Hussain (14)

King Edward VI Handsworth Grammar School For Boys, Handsworth

Hunted

It was life or death. Jeff was stuck in a haunted house while exploring the mysterious forest. He didn't know what was going to happen to him. He had twenty-four hours, when the clock struck twelve he would be murdered.

The only way out was to climb to the peak of the house. Many had attempted, none had succeeded. With skeletons all over the rotten floor, water dripping from the ceiling, eyes of paintings staring at him, ghosts screaming, "You are dead!"

He had to reach the top with everything trying to kill him. Would he ascend to the top?

Saif Samin (11)

King Edward VI Handsworth Grammar School For Boys, Handsworth

Deported

It's not safe now they know. What'll happen to me? I'll be deported.

I've been running for ages. How could my friend betray me? Especially after I told him I'm an illegal immigrant in confidence. Where can I run to? My legs are aching and my back is half broken.

Oh no! A police car with bright lights is pulling up beside me. I can't walk.

"Castillo Benitez, 3572, get in! You're under arrest."

"Sir, please!"

I am surrounded by officers who think I am a threat. I have been stabbed in the back.

Harmanjot Singh (12)
King Edward VI Handsworth Grammar School For Boys, Handsworth

Within The Darkness

In the darkness, my eyes darted from left to right, attempting to make sense of my surroundings. The droplets of water raced down my face, tears or sweat, I didn't know. Both tasted of salt.

The empty darkness consumed me whole, churning me, giving me this feeling of sickness. It felt like there was no way out, as sirens from the distance screamed my name. Suddenly, a deep voice appeared, so deep even the trees shook. But not in fear.

"We are here!"

The soothing crunch of gravel grew into a torment on my brain as it got much closer...

Lewis Goddard (15)
King Edward VI Handsworth Grammar School For Boys, Handsworth

The Mysterious Island

My friend and I just survived a horrific helicopter crash. Upon us lay an island; a peculiar, mysterious land. We struggled to stand up after jumping out of the helicopter. The pain was excruciating, blood was dripping down our legs.

Limping across the island, we came across a tribe of men. They were terrifying, disgust came into my thoughts. They were covered in black mud, like animals, and had hair down to their shoulders.

Transfixed, we continued to stare. My mind was rushing with thoughts, who were they? That's when we realised we were prey.

Karisun Pirapaharan (12)

King Edward VI Handsworth Grammar School For Boys, Handsworth

The Hunter

We were close, tracks of the dragon-like beast littered the ground. The year was 3019, the mutant virus had broken out. Civilisation collapsed; humankind had to hunt or be hunted.

As I trudged on through, the snow pierced my feet like a thousand needles. Me and my hunters clambered to the top... only to find ourselves surrounded by wolves. Their dagger-like teeth oozed yellow goo.

Suddenly, one of the beasts lunged. I knocked the beast off me. The wolves fled; were they scared of us, or what now stood behind us? Red blood littered the ground. Run...

Benjamin Kuffa (11)
King Edward VI Handsworth Grammar School For Boys, Handsworth

The Worst Nightmare

We had twenty-four hours until we were all done for. One winner, one loser. Me and my friends were entrapped and we had just escaped the facility.

We ploughed through the forest and collapsed on the other side. The guards of the facility were shooting their guns at us. My heart was beating and my friends dashed away with me, out of the facility, into the forest.

On the other side, there was a group of people, like dwarves. They had pink-coloured skin and had devilish eyes.

Each inhalation was like a needle stabbing down through my throat. Silence.

Cameron Lai (12)
King Edward VI Handsworth Grammar School For Boys, Handsworth

Loss

I couldn't run much longer... It was just me now, they took all my friends. I wouldn't have got this far without them, but watching as they got caught... I couldn't bear. My heart was urging my legs. I took my last step then collapsed. I was miles away. Could I make it to the safe house and take my chances, or return home and live a normal life?

No. I would carry out my order and friends' wishes - "Finish the mission."

"Get up."

"No!" It couldn't be. He was alive. I saw him... he was caught.

Roneet Shekhar (12)
King Edward VI Handsworth Grammar School For Boys, Handsworth

Revenge Of The Unknown

It wasn't safe anymore. Sitting alone in an abandoned house, Jack's troubled eyes were tired and his body was in excruciating pain.

At the age of fifteen, Jack was recruited by the CIA to prevent the Mafia's plan to steal a billion dollars. He had ended up in Russia, almost killed. In the end, the Mafia failed because of him and they wanted revenge.

On that day, late at night, a postman came to the abandoned house and took out an odd-looking phone. He dialled a few numbers. There was an explosion, and the suspicious postman left without a trace.

Ehan Taseen (12)
King Edward VI Handsworth Grammar School For Boys, Handsworth

Hunted

I couldn't run for much longer, blood was oozing from my wound and I didn't intend on stopping. I could still hear their distant growling as the moon rose, I could sense them coming closer.

I was surrounded by silence. Something was waiting to pounce. I couldn't go any further; it hurt too much. I felt dizzy, I fell to the floor and blacked out.

When I regained consciousness, something was awfully different... *ragh!* I was surrounded by wolves. They bared their teeth like they hadn't eaten in years. I knew I was done for.

Osman Alqaqaa Abdelrahim (11)
King Edward VI Handsworth Grammar School For Boys, Handsworth

Her

One girl, that's all, just one girl. She was... different. She wasn't like the others. Her head was shaved and she had powers. She would give a look and something completely unrelated would move. It would just fly through the air, almost possessed by a force unbeknown to us.

They were like them, completely submerged in secrecy, but they had a desire, a need for her. No one could have her...

A bombardment of gunshots catapulted towards us. All that remained was a faint echoing shriek that surrounded us like a storm. And we were in the eye of it.

Arun Jaswal (15)
King Edward VI Handsworth Grammar School For Boys, Handsworth

Fulfilment

The sirens wailed; the police were here to take me away. I'd finally released all the anger and hate that society gave me. The government acting like they gave a damn about me. The rest of the world looking at me like some kind of freak, some kind of monster.

You feel like society's closing in on you, hunting you. Everyone's judging you, making you feel like you've done something wrong. The anger and the hate builds up. You try to just... keep smiling, but one day, you can't take it. One day, you... snap. And well, what a rush!

Eisa Ali Yacoob (15)

King Edward VI Handsworth Grammar School For Boys, Handsworth

The Hunter

The crimson city became enveloped by thick fog that blinded any survivors. The final thoughts of the fallen screamed throughout the veil as they hung from flickering streetlamps. And at the centre of the chaos stood one, his name forgotten by time, his face lost to insanity. Inscribed on him was every sin known to man, bar the ones inflicted upon him.

Cursed with the burden of eternal life, he scoured the plains, seeking passage onto Earth in order to quench his vast hatred in the only way he knew how - the torture, death and destruction of life.

Adam Khalid Khan (14)

King Edward VI Handsworth Grammar School For Boys, Handsworth

The Apocalypse

Footsteps. It was nearing us...

It was 2087, on a cold December night. The footsteps echoed into the darkness of the lab. Alarms were wailing. It saw us. It ran towards us with great speed and I shut the door to my dimensional teleporter. The zombie horde was here! I whisked off into the multiverse, setting my arm on the controls. My whole body was aching and stinging. I screamed in agonising pain. I landed in an opposite universe; I saw myself as the evil which had corrupted this world.

I stumbled upon a time machine to save all mankind.

Manveer Ballagan (11)

King Edward VI Handsworth Grammar School For Boys, Handsworth

Inevitable

The time is upon us. Years and years of running, hiding from that which many think will elevate their status in society. Lie upon lie - all petty deterrences in the face of the unyielding juggernaut known as time, breaking and cracking like mere twigs.

I thought I had longer to prepare. And in that moment, I had a revelation. All these hours spent avoiding the inevitable could have been used bypassing its internal intimidation tactics. But now I could only watch despairingly, as the juggernaut opened its mouth, revealing the accursed GCSE exams.

Abdul Majid (14)

King Edward VI Handsworth Grammar School For Boys, Handsworth

Hunter's Chase

Midday. The scorching sun had begun to singe the tips of my hair. The sweaty stench spurred me to continue. With every inhalation, the adrenaline rose.

We had planned our surreptitious movement to leave no trace behind. We got closer to the safe point but we were besieged by uniforms. Surpassing the swarms, we continued to endure the non-stop rush.

Miles had built up between us and them. What looked like a dead-end was the finish line. Siren after siren blasted, all entrances emitted a blue aura. We had been set up. We were being hunted.

Raihan Ali (16)
King Edward VI Handsworth Grammar School For Boys, Handsworth

Targeted

It's not safe now they know. I can distinctly hear footsteps approaching my direction. The rifles constantly click, frantically; I can't escape the sound.
My tail alertly coiled up like a yo-yo whilst I gaze continuously through the gaps in the trees that encroach on me. My territory intruded, my life on the line. Where can I go?
It is time. I have to engage my instincts and guard, gravely, my past, present and future. I embed my piercing claws into the flaccid Earth. At this moment in time, I am a deer in headlights. I am being hunted.

Christopher Lee (16)
King Edward VI Handsworth Grammar School For Boys, Handsworth

Robbery Of Billions!

Sirens wailed and people cried in the distance. The hunt had just begun. This is how it all started...

It was twelve o'clock at night and the bank was closed. There were no signs of any passers-by. Me and my gang rushed straight to the bank, destroying the supposedly strong glass, broke into the safe and stole the millions - or even billions - of pounds. Then burned down the bank and ran off.

Now, red and blue beaming lights were two metres away from me and my gang. Suddenly, a police car confronted us. It was too late, we were caught.

Harvey Nandra (11)

King Edward VI Handsworth Grammar School For Boys, Handsworth

Last Days Of My Life

I was panting heavily, knowing I might not have a tomorrow. I scurried towards a grey, diseased bush. I quickly regained my strength and started sprinting, thinking what would happen if I halted.

I was being followed by three cruel human beings. I had been in this situation for four days, wondering what they would do to me. Sweat was dripping off my arms and legs. At this point, I thought I was going to collapse. But I had the determination inside me to carry on.

I went behind a half-broken brick wall to relax. How would this ever end?

Shiven Singh (11)
King Edward VI Handsworth Grammar School For Boys, Handsworth

A New Life

Bullets ripped past my face as I ran toward the forest. Men shouted from my past life, that's when the gate erected from the ground. My hope for freedom disappeared in front of my eyes.

Deceitful demons drove their black bikes towards me like hyenas edging closer to a cub. Growling and snarling at me, they were telling me to stop but they never knew me, not well enough.

Lightning ruptured throughout my body while flashbangs blew up around me. The only light in this darkness. Over the gate, I reached my destination. Everlasting freedom.

Nyrun Hargun (16)
King Edward VI Handsworth Grammar School For Boys, Handsworth

Confusion

Everyone was frozen. Everyone in my class acted as robots, each with a blue, flashing tint in their eyes. Word by word, everyone was speaking simultaneously.

I felt as if I was hallucinating, however, now wasn't the time to think about that. Why wasn't I speaking along with them? I caught a glimpse from the corner of my eye, of our teacher tapping on a tablet. Each tap causing my peers to speak another language.

It was as if everything about them had become sucked out and replaced with a machine. Then the teacher noticed me...

Armaan Hussain (14)

King Edward VI Handsworth Grammar School For Boys, Handsworth

The Great Escape

I couldn't run for much longer, every step I took felt like a piece of my leg crumbling off until my legs were no more. Sirens wailed in the distance, police searching for a lifeless man - me.

As I went through a bush, prickly thorns stabbed me all over. I dragged my feet along the ground, hoping they wouldn't find me. The sirens started fading away.

I took a sigh of relief but my sense still felt danger, making me shudder. I wanted to stop but my instincts kept me going for some unknown reason, sending chills down my spine.

Taha Umar (11)
King Edward VI Handsworth Grammar School For Boys, Handsworth

Taking A Risk

The sirens wailed. They weren't far. I ploughed through the bushes, trying to evade the chase. I thought I couldn't run anymore. "This is it," I told myself.

Out of nowhere, my friend raced through the forest with a car. "Get in now," he exclaimed.

I got in; I'd barely escaped. "What took you so long?" I asked him.

"You're welcome," he replied.

My heart was racing. I'd finally escaped! Or so I thought.

A car pulled out in front of us. We hit it. The person got out and directed both of us to his car. We'd been hunted.

Arjun Sohanpal (11)
King Edward VI Handsworth Grammar School For Boys, Handsworth

Soul Hunter Strikes

All I remember is that I was a kid yesterday, now I'm a thirty-two-year-old killing machine. The reason I'm a killing machine is because I killed mastermind Vincenzo Bonebody. Apparently, he tried to blow up the Burj Khalifa. If climbing it using your bare hands isn't exhilarating enough, what else could be? Being a colonel in the army, he knew which kind of grenades and bombs to use.

As he was approaching in his Lamborghini (he was rich), I shot his tyre, sending him into his own bomb and blowing him up. That's all a day's work.

Pravit Vashisht (11)

King Edward VI Handsworth Grammar School For Boys, Handsworth

Nerve Agent

I was running, running for my life and the lives of my city, my home. I had just managed to escape the guards, taking the only bottle of nerve-agent with me. Instantly, the alarm went off. I heard ear-splitting shouts and, from a glance, I knew I was being hunted. My head was aching, my arms and legs densely covered in large, painful blisters. As I approached the field, at the end of which was the police station, I was filled with great anxiety. Would I make it? I bolted rapidly, nothing but my adrenaline was continuously urging me on.

Eran Luyima (11)
King Edward VI Handsworth Grammar School For Boys, Handsworth

Everywhere But Nowhere

Someone had been watching me, but why? I was on the run because of this; I didn't want to disappear like my uncle did. I had no home, I wouldn't stay for long anywhere until now. On the edge of London, I saw this house which was never lit. I pondered about sleeping there, only for the night, until morning.

Legs like jelly, feet trembling and teeth chattering, how could I get inside? I scanned for threats in the dusty house, silently and cautiously.

I saw a woman holding a cricket bat. I heard a tick... *boom!*

Hardev Manku (12)

King Edward VI Handsworth Grammar School For Boys, Handsworth

The House

My bones were aching. My toes were numb. I couldn't run anymore - until I heard it. It screamed, "I can see you," in a creepy voice that reminded me of a horror movie.
I ran down the street until I reached an official-looking house. I ran to it. But suddenly, everything changed. The place was deserted, I was on my own. I went around, looking around the house. It seemed perfectly normal until I went in. The house looked really old, then I entered a bedroom. I had an immensely heavy feeling that I was not alone in there...

Muhammed Nasim Ahmed
King Edward VI Handsworth Grammar School For Boys, Handsworth

Enter

I walked through the alleyway. I didn't know why, but I knew he told me to come here. Rain pounded on my once-perfect hair. *Beep!*

My life flashed before my eyes. I was knocked onto the floor, people with sharp knives gathered around me, mumbling words I couldn't understand.

Suddenly, a man in a hoodie lifted me and put me into a bag. After what seemed like hours, I was dropped in front of a rusty door. I knew I had to enter.

I went into a dank, musty room and looked around. But then I started feeling nauseous...

Tinron Chan (11)
King Edward VI Handsworth Grammar School For Boys, Handsworth

Russian Race

The moon shone its spotlight on the snowy roads, early morning yawning from the Japanese seas. A Jaguar blurred past, kicking the snow into a fury.

Ahmed looked behind him, no Ladas. He was relieved until the gunfire pounced at him. The Ladas pounced at him, running for their prey.

Ahmed stepped all his fright onto the accelerator, gripping the steering wheel. It should be the CIA in this position - they were too busy with Castro.

The bullets leapt onto the back of the car, a hand reaching to pull the car into darkness...

Raahil Junaid (14)
King Edward VI Handsworth Grammar School For Boys, Handsworth

Midnight!

One night, I was wandering through the forest with my mates. Midnight. I heard wolves and owls. I couldn't get to sleep, I'd decided to go for a walk with the others as they were witnessing the same problem.

We walked for ten minutes, then decided to go back. We were lost. Whilst trying to find a way back, I heard the wolves' noises getting closer. I saw them. We began to run. Running as fast as I could, I tripped. The wolves gained on me; I was surrounded. All my friends had gone. They pounced. This was the end...

Jay Gaddu (11)

King Edward VI Handsworth Grammar School For Boys, Handsworth

Guilty

I grasped onto as much oxygen as I possibly could; my breaths getting deeper and deeper every time I took a stride. Sirens wailed, closing in on me.

The night sky was coloured with red and blue lights. I could sense the people staring at me through their windows, my black hoodie was drenched in sweat from fear and exhaustion. But I had to keep going.

I looked at my bloody hands, beginning to slow down. I couldn't tell whether my face was full of tears or sweat. I suddenly clutched my left rib in pain. I collapsed in shock.

Mustapha Haris (14)
King Edward VI Handsworth Grammar School For Boys, Handsworth

WWIII Escape

It was December 15th 2019 when World War III broke out. I was on a holiday in England and was staying at my friend Abdul's house. We were just playing some FIFA, until our doorbell chimed.

Some soldiers were standing at the door. They demanded us to evacuate. We rapidly packed our bags. Abdul got his keys to his Ferrari 488 Pista. As we got in the car, Abdul sped off. As we arrived at Dover, we were told to stop by the army. But they didn't have an English flag on their uniforms. It was the enemy - the Russian army...

Muhammad Moosa Raza (11)
King Edward VI Handsworth Grammar School For Boys, Handsworth

The Run

Beep! The sirens wailed; the chase was on. I couldn't feel the blood leaking out of my shoulder anymore. Sweat rolled down my skin in thick, salty beads. My feet pounded the tarmac with all the grace of a sack of wet concrete, the springing graceful steps of twenty miles earlier had long since disappeared.

My rasping throat was as parched as a dead lizard in the desert sun. My head bobbed loosely from side to side with each footfall and my eyes felt heavy in their sockets. I wheezed as my burning lungs gasped for air.

Zayan Arshad (12)
King Edward VI Handsworth Grammar School For Boys, Handsworth

Hunted

As the beam of sunlight was waiting to be engulfed by the never-ending swirl of darkness, I left school. The huge buzz of chattering had gone, all I could hear now was the tranquillity of the birds twittering and the owls hooting. But, at that moment, I wouldn't realise that the calmness of the night would suddenly change. It all changed when I realised there was something following me. The red glow in their eyes was all I could see of this figure. Every turn, they turned.

It was at this moment that I realised I'd become the prey.

Hamza Arif (12)
King Edward VI Handsworth Grammar School For Boys, Handsworth

Freedom

I'd got a few hundred metres away from the wretched prison before the alarms blared throughout the facility, sounding like air-raid sirens. In the blink of an eye, blinding floodlights shone around the place and the deafening barks of the guard dogs echoed in the night.

My legs were on fire but I knew they were tracking me down quickly, wanting to take me back. Soon enough, a wave of wailing sirens flooded my hearing and I knew I had to make my escape.

Being free for a day was one hundred times better than staying there.

Anthony Simon Maczka (15)
King Edward VI Handsworth Grammar School For Boys, Handsworth

Wanted

I'd been running for days to escape the horror which lay behind me. They were closing in with every passing second. My legs burnt but I had to keep moving.

As I jumped over the trees' claw-like feet, I noticed it was quiet. Too quiet. I stopped and reached for my gun as the eerie silence loomed over me.

I heard a faint voice in the distance. They were close. I began sprinting for my life and tripped over a root, falling face-first into the wet forest floor. Torches began to illuminate my form.

I'd been caught...

Amaan Siddique (15)
King Edward VI Handsworth Grammar School For Boys, Handsworth

They're Coming

I couldn't run for much longer. I looked around the temple and there it was - the escape portal. I hurried in, trying to forget the sins I'd committed.

I stepped out of the portal, only to see mysterious figures lurking around in the darkness of that sinister world. I tried to run to the portal but then they came. I knew that they wouldn't stop until they found me.

I managed to run to the portal. They chased me and, when I tripped, I woke up.

I looked outside but I saw them. This couldn't be real. Or was it?

Ahmed Osman (11)
King Edward VI Handsworth Grammar School For Boys, Handsworth

Border Patrol

Sirens wailed from all directions. I had thirty minutes to reach the border, otherwise it would be on full lockdown. I hid in some bushes, hoping to lose the police but they still found me. The wire fence behind me had a small hole in it, so I clambered through.

Oddly, the grass was blue, the sky was purple... I had no idea what was going on. I was in an unearthly realm but I was still able to hear the sirens.

My throat tightened, shooting pains were flowing in my ribs. Therefore I couldn't run for much longer...

Callum Mann (11)
King Edward VI Handsworth Grammar School For Boys, Handsworth

Sea Of Red

For now, let me start at the beginning...
On a lonely highway, just me and the car. Until my car broke
down - very unusual for that to occur. I heard a massive
splash! A huge lake was quite nearby. So I investigated with
a flashlight from the car.
As I travelled toward the lake, I witnessed an entity
emerging out of the lake. There were several others as well.
The gruesome monsters glanced over at me. And they came.
I ran as fast as I could but they caught up. Their roars
echoed in the night. I kept running.

Ismaeel Ali (11)
King Edward VI Handsworth Grammar School For Boys, Handsworth

Wanted...

He sat there, listening to the fire crackling. He was a wanted criminal who had murdered more than fifty innocent citizens and stolen from the bank more than twice. There was a reason for these terrible actions. When he was young, he and his mum fled their country for England. Along the way his mother died, having been shot by a bullet some miles away. He mourned her and swore revenge on the man who killed her. Out of anger, he committed these actions.
He snapped back to reality as the sirens wailed; he had to leave, now!

Abdul Rehman (11)
King Edward VI Handsworth Grammar School For Boys, Handsworth

Lost

Location: lost in a different universe. Date: unknown. Time: evening.

We were close. Very close. I could see it from a distance - an ordinary house. The residents could be one of us or one of them. This was a deadly lottery.

We approached the door. Ryan, my best friend, knocked. There was an awkward silence. Nothing. We tried again, this time I knocked.

It's amazing how you can feel so lonely in such a large crowd of people. Just as we were about to leave, I heard it. Footsteps. The doorknob turned and it pounced...

Arjun Lyall (12)

King Edward VI Handsworth Grammar School For Boys, Handsworth

The Chase

My legs ached; my head made it feel like agony every time it moved. But I knew I couldn't stop running. *Crackle!* I knew they were after me.

Sprinting every second I could, trying to use my speed against them, I stared into the darkness, not knowing if I would ever see the light of day again. The feeling was exhilarating, much like a game of Tag - but I was playing with Death himself. I heard a shriek. The feeling of hysteria overwhelmed me. I didn't know if I would make it out alive until I heard his voice...

Chetan Dhami (12)
King Edward VI Handsworth Grammar School For Boys, Handsworth

Hunted

His heart raced; he had just committed an unforgivable crime but it gave him a thrill. A thrill he could've never had otherwise. He ran. As he hyperventilated, just like an owl he looked back. He saw two things: the consequences of his action and a herd of police charging at him. He was being hunted! From the moment he did it, he knew this would happen. He broke the... a moral taboo. He had killed a man. He was a bloodthirsty psychopath, a maniac, and as he realised this, he fell to this knees, knowing he had been caught.

John Obayelu (11)
King Edward VI Handsworth Grammar School For Boys, Handsworth

The Trapdoor

The sirens wailed as my foot stepped out of the isolated cell, guards came running in like a pack of hyenas, bloodthirsty for their prey. I hadn't thought this through; so I just ran like my life depended on it. It was inevitable that I would get caught but my mind focused on a door, it was sliding down. I still had a chance to escape out of this rust-ridden prison. I jumped over the stairs so gracefully that even the guards stopped in awe.

I slid under just in time. At last, I was free. But being hunted down...

Mohammad Bilal Ahmad (16)
King Edward VI Handsworth Grammar School For Boys, Handsworth

By Dragon's Bane

We had to leave. It was that or die. I could hear the hunting dogs howling at us. Either we died by tooth or blade. We had no choice.

"Amber, we need to land," I screeched over the howling wind.

Amber soared to the ground and was bombarded by arrows. Amber, the kind dragon who was joined to my heart became a killing machine. She slaughtered soldiers with malice and glee. She turned to me with an intense look in her eyes. She bounded toward me, teeth bared. I ran from the slaughter. I was prey. I was hunted.

Oliver Fance (12)
King Edward VI Handsworth Grammar School For Boys, Handsworth

The Phone Call

Pain. Fear. Adrenaline. I had to block it out; there was no time for it. My brain pulled every exit, distraction, anything, to help me get out. Why? Because I had to. I spun around, right into the guy. Whilst apologising, I managed to pinch his phone. I slipped out of my coat to alter my appearance. Cameras seemed to watch my moves. I made my way towards the door. The guards had been stunned. I managed to disappear. Every step I took made me feel better. But then the phone rang. A phone call that would change my life.

Muhammad Amir Zaier (16)
King Edward VI Handsworth Grammar School For Boys, Handsworth

The Lingerer

They were looking for my blood. Like a great white shark roaming the sea. I would never forget that face, a balaclava covering it, only cut out to show his scars and tattoos. *Bang!* A bullet skimmed my shoulder... Oh no, it was him. The predator. He crept up on me, tugged me by my shirt. It felt like his fist had lingered in the air for minutes. Then... contact.

He started to grab out a blade and proceeded to rip along my torso. Then he took the balaclava off. It was... wait a second, my dad? Why?

Erjon Beqiri (11)

King Edward VI Handsworth Grammar School For Boys, Handsworth

Welcome To The Jungle

I can't run for much longer. My name is Ajay Phull and I'm currently being hunted by a Titanosaurus. I have nearly died five times in five days. I take a quick drink from my flask. I look up at the sky and shout, "Why me?" I stalk over to the river and refill my flask. Then I notice a door.
I walk cautiously over to it, my curiosity getting the better of me yet again. Just then, I stop. I turn around and see a humongous beast looking down at me, hungrily. I turn and am plunged into darkness.

Ajay Phull (11)
King Edward VI Handsworth Grammar School For Boys, Handsworth

Exit From Earth

In the upcoming hour, it was almost certain that he would be found by the authorities. He had nowhere left to hide; he was out of chances and now he would become one of them. Another outcast. There was absolutely no chance of redemption, for he had taken this lie too far. The doors were shut but were going to blast open anytime soon, symbolising his exit from normality. So sudden, so unexpected. It wasn't his fault but it was too late to confess now. He was in purgatory, waiting to be dragged to the fires of Hell.

Arjun Kalirai (15)
King Edward VI Handsworth Grammar School For Boys, Handsworth

The Beast

It was onto me. It was gaining. It was going to catch me. I weaved in and out of trees, under and over the branches. I couldn't run forever.

The moon was glowing and the wind was howling. I was almost out of the pitch-black woods when I heard a noise. "*Owwow!*" It was coming. My heart skipped a beat. I scanned the area, nothing! I carried on and I raced past the fallen trees, but then I felt a smash like a plane hitting my back. All I could see now was black. All just plain black.

Abdullah Faisal Jamil (11)
King Edward VI Handsworth Grammar School For Boys, Handsworth

Haunted Doll

I still have nightmares about the haunted doll that followed me. I felt like the haunted doll was going to murder me. I needed someone to stay behind with me because I was really scared that the haunted doll was going to do something to me.

The next day, I went to the local police station and asked the police officer if he could help me. He said, "Why do you need my help?"

I said, "A creepy doll is following me everywhere and I want you to stop her."

Then the creepy doll appeared...

Jashandeep Singh (11)

King Edward VI Handsworth Grammar School For Boys, Handsworth

Apocalypse

I was close to the end. I had fifteen minutes to save the world from the zombie apocalypse.

I turned right at the end of the corridor and, with the corner of my eye, I had a glimpse of the infamous assassin: the Red Wolf. I was petrified as I saw the sniper that could be the last thing I ever saw.

"Hello, 782964, how are you? How does it feel to live?"

Panic started to swarm up in my mind but I knew that even the slightest of movements could get me killed. I didn't know what to do...

Hamthan Farish (12)

King Edward VI Handsworth Grammar School For Boys, Handsworth

The Escape

We were close to the den when we heard rustling in the bushes. Suddenly, men with dogs appeared. I had only one option, to run. This had started when I broke out of jail for being mistakenly accused of theft. These dogs were rapid. I couldn't run much more when I thought of the back-up den. The bushes were extremely hurtful. The back-up den had only a little space. I had finally arrived when a gun was pointed at my head. I tried to escape with all my might. I broke free, and that was when I heard it...

Yousuf Assaf Bashir (11)
King Edward VI Handsworth Grammar School For Boys, Handsworth

Hide Or Die

We never knew we had twenty-four hours. Me and my friends knew we were cursed, but we never thought that the devil was after us. We were running for our lives, trying to find a way out. No chance! The monsters closed in, our only option was to fight. We used the weapons we chose, mine was a golden sword and the others had bows and arrows. We charged. One, two of our team gobbled by these horrors. Me holding strong until... we were edged onto a cliff. One push and we were dead. Would they? Surely... they would!

Rayaan Iqbal (12)
King Edward VI Handsworth Grammar School For Boys, Handsworth

Never Be Safe

I would never be safe. Not when I was forced to hide like this. It might've been time for me to rethink my actions. Did I have to anger them? At least it was a good cause. I carried on running, naturally. My peril was inevitable. I continued, as if I had a chance.

I looked behind my shoulder... nothing! Then I saw it. I looked back in front of me. They were there, right there! Not thinking straight, I carried on running.

I then saw who I thought to be my saviour. He grinned. How could he betray me?

Diego Kerr (11)
King Edward VI Handsworth Grammar School For Boys, Handsworth

Instinct

A frantic left turn, a drift to the right - I couldn't keep ahead much longer. I panicked as the killswitch from the helicopter began to get a lock on my vehicle. I risked some of my precious nitro' to propel me out of range.

With half the cops after me, stopping was a luxury I couldn't afford. Unless I could find a bypass to get out of the circle of police cars attempting to pull me in, my life would be over. My failures would overtake me and my passion, which had kept me safe, would be destroyed.

Ahmed Patel (15)

King Edward VI Handsworth Grammar School For Boys, Handsworth

The Hunter Becomes The Hunted

I wanted to kill him. I wanted him to die a long, painful death. I wanted him to be eaten by cockroaches. I was in a place I knew he wasn't gonna come to - his own house. An hour later, I heard footsteps, then a growl. I loaded my AR-15 and stood in front of the door.

As soon as the door opened, *bang!* In the chest. *Bang!* In the brain. *Bang!* In the heart. I then said, "Get ready for the longest sleep you've ever had, because the hunter has become the hunted."

Aryan Singh Kular (11)

King Edward VI Handsworth Grammar School For Boys, Handsworth

Run!

We had to leave. We had to leave now. It was crawling through the vents, ready to kill. We knew if we stopped running we'd regret it. I could feel the creature's will to kill. There was a bang on the floor. Billy had collapsed. The creature leapt out of the vent, blood poured all over the decaying floor. I couldn't go back, I ran. I felt my utter shame as I sprinted towards the shattered window. I smashed it more, jumped through it and hid. I had lost my best friend but just about escaped with my own life.

Jai Whitehouse (12)
King Edward VI Handsworth Grammar School For Boys, Handsworth

The Hunter

It began in 3001. An ill-famed man, John Martin, appeared uninvitedly to this town. This man was no common man. This man had a hook at the end of his arm, which he used to mercilessly kill and murder people who he called sinners. John was given many names, such as Blackhood, but he was most well-known as The Hunter. He was known for taking people into his basement and torturing them day and night. How do you know so much, you may ask? Well, my real name is Mr Martin, but I'd like you to call me John.

Rafiad Choudhury (12)

King Edward VI Handsworth Grammar School For Boys, Handsworth

No Time Left

Watching, smelling and listening, I darted along the cold, pillow-like snow. My desire only to get away from what must be the end. It never used to be like this, and now the tides have changed. I'm not in the shallow but in the murky depths of the deep. I had to keep running for my life, for my family. But how could I? Every step felt like stepping into lava and every breath nearly killed me.

I heard a cold, sinister breath behind me. Oh no, he had found me. The great wolf, yes, he had found me.

Michael Matthew White (11)
King Edward VI Handsworth Grammar School For Boys, Handsworth

Hunted

I heard the ticking. I was close to completing my mission but someone had other ideas. That someone was my father, Roger Stevens. I hate my father. He's the most sinister person you could ever see. He wanted to steal the magic clock and use it for his own evil purposes. Who would win this hunt for the clock? I was going to find out in about ten seconds. That's when I saw him. My father had won. He had the clock and he used it to make a portal to another universe. I was sucked inside the portal forever.

Ibaad Qureshi (11)

King Edward VI Handsworth Grammar School For Boys, Handsworth

The Chase Was On!

I was exhausted. I couldn't run for much longer. I think I was the last one left! I looked to the left and the right. Was I safe? Wait... what was that? I felt something or someone breathing down my neck. I slowly turned around to find... him. My old teammate. He was a double agent! He was looking for me! He dragged me across the field, shooting all the enemies that came in his way. Sprinting as fast as he could, dodging all of the bullets, he ran to the escape chopper and quickly jumped inside of it.

Joshan Kudhail (12)
King Edward VI Handsworth Grammar School For Boys, Handsworth

Spied... On

I couldn't run for much longer. Where could I go? I was being chased by spies. I was on the run.

Many hours passed and I had been surviving off fresh berries in a nearby forest where I had found an abandoned shack. This would be where I would stay for the next few weeks until they would abandon their mission. Or would they? I could be stranded here for the rest of my life.

Days later, I heard murmurs in the distance. I saw flickers of light. They had caught up to me. They had spied on me...

Max Ho (12)
King Edward VI Handsworth Grammar School For Boys, Handsworth

The End

Where can I hide? I am well out of the city. It's been a while since I stopped running. Unfortunately, the police are still after me; I heard the loud, wailing noise of a helicopter going past. I keep telling myself I'll be alright, but something in my head was telling me the truth - I had killed her. My stepmother. What have I done? My heart is still pumping rapidly as if it wants to escape my body. Sweat is pouring down from my head onto my collar. My body is filled with fear. I think it's the end.

Amin Mohammad Khakssar (11)
King Edward VI Handsworth Grammar School For Boys, Handsworth

My Last Chance

I knew I shouldn't have but my curiosity got the better of me. Cautious of everything around me, I slowly went up the stairs. I reached the top, in front of me stood a long, thin hallway. Suddenly, a big bang occurred. With no time to lose, I sprinted as fast as I could go. I reached a dead-end. The figure appeared, carrying a knife. I had very little time until I was dead.The moment he aimed the knife at me, I darted past. I couldn't run for much longer, I smashed the window and jumped out.

Yusef Hakim (12)
King Edward VI Handsworth Grammar School For Boys, Handsworth

Murder

I couldn't run for much longer. They were still chasing me. I didn't know why, but the town came after me.

I woke up in a strange lab, full of bodies on the floor. They were dead. That was how I got here, running from insane policemen. I had become the prey.

I kept running, the nettles were tearing at my skin which made me slower. Then running became jogging, then jogging became walking, then walking became crawling. I found an old house on the horizon. I tried to crawl to it.

Mohammad Shayan (11)
King Edward VI Handsworth Grammar School For Boys, Handsworth

Not Good Enough

Every step I take feels like the last. Droplets of sweat race down my face as I wait, silently. The ice-cold air burns my insides but the adrenaline only lessens the pain. Carbon dioxide puffs out of me in great clouds like a steam train. Even worse, my legs begin to ache and cramp - the pain forcing me to rest since it is so unbearable.

A few moments later, I look down at the dark forest floor to plan my next movements carefully. I force my right foot forward, *snap!*

Neil Chen (16)

King Edward VI Handsworth Grammar School For Boys, Handsworth

Restless

The heels of my feet turn my white socks a crimson-red. As they bleed, thread on the side of my face becomes undone and the face of the guard falls off my head. Discarding the skin, I keep moving. I can't be caught. My body pleads for a moment of rest but time is not a luxury I have. Every breath burns my dry throat. The heat feels like a blazing inferno. I reach a path and follow it to the outside world. I approach a woman for directions; she screams. I still have no face.

Ritish Sadhra (16)
King Edward VI Handsworth Grammar School For Boys, Handsworth

The Experimental Disaster

I couldn't run for much longer. The last of the remaining limbs I had ached. The sirens started; the hunt had begun, and I was the prey. I knew they were tracking me down now. They were close, I could sense it. No, I thought, I can't go back. I wasn't going back to the lab to have another limb cut off.

I limped over to a bush nearby. They were right in front of me, I was two inches away from death or worse. They walked off. I was safe. But not for long...

Zakariya Nawaz (11)

King Edward VI Handsworth Grammar School For Boys, Handsworth

Hitman

Where can I hide? I am wanted, I am being hunted by a hitman. It's been weeks since I went back home. My wound is starting to heal.

It was a Friday night at 9pm, a man approached me. He was crossing his arms in such a way, that his hands were in his pockets. When I figured out what was in his pocket, it was too late. He slashed his blade across my face, cutting my eye. *Bang!* The man died, then a familiar man glanced back at me.

Osman Yahia (11)

King Edward VI Handsworth Grammar School For Boys, Handsworth

The Long Haul

I can't run for much longer. Once, I was top-of-the-line. Now considered obsolete. My T-2599 chassis wasn't made for the conditions of a harsh desert wasteland.

System check: knee joints, two thousand grains of sand in, ninety-three pushed out. This has been the case, in varying numbers, for the past three days.

Calculation... eleven hours until leg functions become ineffective. Calculation... ten hours and thirty-two minutes system time required for system recalibration of upper and lower exo-skeletal arms.

Once legs are ineffective, estimated travel distance in this form... 572 miles. Desert calculations: desert area squared... 1256 miles.

Oliver Bailey (13)
The Wigston Academies Trust, Wigston

Wanted

"Have we spotted her yet?" I said.

"I see a shape in the mist, sir. I think that's Bristol," said Petty Officer Baker. "She seems a few miles off, we should surface to release the fumes and start our route to Bristol..." When we made it to about one hundred metres, we began to make radio contact.

"Hello, this is HMS Bristol. What do you want?" said the man on the radio.

"This is HMS Alliance. Please surrender our ship before we begin a full-scale attack."

"What?" said the radio. "Why?"

"Because I know we're not allies," I said.

Merlin Otto Lee (12)
The Wigston Academies Trust, Wigston

Hunted

"They're coming!" wailed Chris. "Zombies!"

As Chris and his friend Max ran for their lives, the zombies chased them.

"We're being hunted!" Screamed Max. "Over there! A building! We can hide from them."

They both ran into the building and slammed the door, then locked it.

"We won't make it out alive," cried Chris.

"There's a window, we can escape this building without them knowing."

They jumped out of the window and quietly escaped. They stumbled upon dead bodies and still carried on running.

"Let's climb over the fence," Max snapped.

"No, we don't have enough time. Let's fight them..."

Sukhman Bajwa (12)
The Wigston Academies Trust, Wigston

Hunted

Playing out with my friends, pitch-black, we approached the house. Completely abandoned, it was like a maze. After five minutes of scanning the place, there was a bang. All the doors locked, a loudspeaker played, "You have twenty-four hours to escape, otherwise you owe me your life!"
I ran around everywhere, my friends followed. I was looking for literally anything: clues, ideas that could help me to try and escape. There were five doors, it looked like they needed keys. I searched every cupboard, every room, everything. Two hours in, no keys. There was nowhere else to search.

Riley Grycuk (12)
The Wigston Academies Trust, Wigston

All Or Nothing

Eighty-five minutes in, the score was 4-4. Somehow, we managed to come back from four down. We were fighters. Our situation was simple: win or my childhood club goes bust. I was playing through excruciating pain. My knees couldn't do anymore but I pushed on.

Racing down the wing, an appalling challenge from the defender brought me to a crashing heap on the floor. I was howling in pain but by the time I was up, it was injury time. Matthews' free-kick ricocheted off the crossbar. Instinctively, I dived for it. The defender swung for it... my body was broken.

Cameron Lee (13)
The Wigston Academies Trust, Wigston

Hunted

I've got thirty minutes to reach the border. I am a British Council officer, I'm on holiday in Iraq. They're not happy with me, they say Britain's taken their clean water. Somehow they found out who I am.

I'm on the run to Iran so they don't kill me. The rebels are hunting me down with rocket launchers, AK47s and grenades. There are hundreds of them. I am currently in a little shack, hiding. I hear, "Fire."

A rocket comes flying through the window and gunfire starts all around. I have concussion. They shoot me dead. Goodbye, farewell.

Kane Munday (13)
The Wigston Academies Trust, Wigston

Bad Romance

It's a dangerous world out there, especially now they know. A werewolf could never love a vampire, it's not right. If they catch us, all hell would break loose.

There we were, running in the moonlight, not looking back. Searching for a safe hideout but our bodies were aching. We still heard them calling us in the distance but we ignored them and kept moving.

Our fear turned into anger and frustration as all we wanted was to be together. But the frustration turned back into fear as the distant voices weren't as distant anymore - they were catching up, fast.

Alyssa Eve Vaja (13)
The Wigston Academies Trust, Wigston

Trauma, Trauma Of Andrea Dellora

Screams echoed throughout the hallways, my friends' bodies surrounded me. Closer and closer he crept, his eyes fixed on me, examining me with malicious intent. I wasted no time and ran, with no urge to look back. I thought I knew the school layout, how wrong I was. Turn after turn, door after door; I reached a dead-end. *Thump. Thump.* Heavy footsteps became louder. I couldn't run for much longer. I vaulted through a classroom window and crept around the desks. He found me. *Thud. Thud. Thud...* Then silence. Sharp pains shot through my exhausted body. Blank.

Isabelle Tait (13)
The Wigston Academies Trust, Wigston

The Fast 'N' Furious Saga

The sirens wailed. The engines roared as the tyres screeched. The car raced around the corner and the police followed behind. Noise filled the area, deafening sounds of tyres and sirens.

Drifting around the corner, the metallic grey car reached a dead-end. Police covered all exits. The driver put his foot to the metal and accelerated into a doughnut, forming a cloud of dust which blanketed the vision of the car.

Standing still and ready like a hungry lion waiting to pounce on its prey, the car downshifted into reverse, down the hill, in hope to survive falling.

Rhys Holyland (11)
The Wigston Academies Trust, Wigston

Wounded

Olivia watched as Adelaide hobbled ahead of the rapidly advancing barrier. The wall of spikes was a few seconds from skewering her when she launched herself sideways into a door.

She fell back as the wall's sides grazed against the metal doorframe, raining sparks to the concrete floor. Fire-starters showered into the room and she kicked the door shut with a bang! She fell back.

Her legs spread out across the cold floor and her chest heaved. Her head lolled as she watched a camera in the corner of the room swivel to see her, the blinking light mocking her.

Bethany Fothergill (16)
The Wigston Academies Trust, Wigston

The Sanderson Estate Mystery

It was a dark, hallowed night and I was walking home. Everything was swell until I passed the Sanderson estate. In the past, I was friends with the Sandersons. I decided to pay a visit and walked into the estate courtyard.

After a while, I reached the door. I was greeted by a man with wispy hair; he grabbed me and pulled me into the house, slamming the hefty door behind him. I noticed four graves outside and asked whose they were.

He replied, "The Sandersons'."

Petrified, I ran towards the rear door. He pursued. Now I was being hunted.

Luca Franco Moroni (13)

The Wigston Academies Trust, Wigston

Our Chance

This was our only chance. We had to move. Now. The guards were on change over. Meaning I would have approximately two minutes to escape this concentration camp.

I grabbed as many people as I could and sprinted to the hole in the fence. One minute left. I fell to the floor, crawling through. Eliezer was last. He crawled but got caught in the wire.

"Help!" He screamed, with tears running down his face. We came to his rescue.

Ten seconds. As quick as we possibly could, we untangled his rags. Eliezer was free. We ran and ran.

What next?

Ruby Heathcote (12)
The Wigston Academies Trust, Wigston

Captured

I couldn't run much longer. My sight was fading away. I slapped my face repeatedly to keep my vision in sight. It wasn't working.

I looked for a place to hide, gasping for air; I needed more time. Footsteps were headed towards me, getting louder and louder. I panicked and ran straight ahead of me. The only thing that kept me going was my adrenaline.

Heavy breathing sounds came from behind me. The real hunt was on. Sounds of blades spinning around the air, lights searching for the last one left. And finally, the light stopped in one place: here.

Chi La (12)
The Wigston Academies Trust, Wigston

Running From The Beast

I couldn't run for much longer. My legs were burning and I could hardly breathe, or see anything through the darkness of the forest. Sikha had found me after only one week. Struggling to make my way through the trees, I tripped and fell over a log. But when I opened my eyes, Sikha was standing there towering over me.

"Before you kill me, I would like to know one thing," I mumbled.

"And what is that?" Sikha shouted.

"Why have you hunted me for all these years?" I asked.

"Because you killed my father!"

"... your father isn't dead."

Holly Derbyshire (13)

The Wigston Academies Trust, Wigston

Inside Or Out?

Deep in my dark, isolated and abandoned soul, something isn't right. Is it me or the creature controlling me? With every breath I take, wondering these dreadful thoughts, consuming my mind with every second.

I have yet to decide whether the problem lays within me or deeper. As people start to realise the changes outside, I felt that my insides were going to explode with guilt and dreadful desires.

As the creature hunted down my soul, as I lost my loved ones around me, I released all my tension, anger and fear and let it take over. Who am I?

Molly Hanney (13) & Marissa Faye McFarlane (12)
The Wigston Academies Trust, Wigston

Trapped

Ear-piercing screams filled the air; I desperately needed to escape. Rapidly running, I searched for an exit. Windows? Barred. Doors? Locked. Corridors? Never-ending.
For the first time in forever, I saw humans. But then I realised the bodies were lifeless. Gunshots fired, followed by deafening screams. I knew if I didn't leave, I'd be next.
I grabbed a chair and attacked the window. When I heard it crack, it only needed a few more hits. With all my strength, I smashed the window. Without hesitation, I jumped, not looking back.

Natasha Taylor (13)
The Wigston Academies Trust, Wigston

Alone (I Think)

I escaped. There's no doubt they will come back, but I'm safe for now.

Why doesn't anybody understand that I didn't kill Lily? Just because we didn't get along, doesn't mean I would do something like this. I'm eighteen and I want to be a police officer, what future police officer would commit murder? What was that? It's probably a fox. I'm in the middle of a forest! Do foxes talk? That's a silly question... it's probably me imagining things.

What's that big scar on my leg? Why on Earth is there a cold hand sitting on my shoulder?

Hannah Bigden (11)
The Wigston Academies Trust, Wigston

Run!

It was a dark, eerie night when me and three of my friends got kidnapped by two guys in a black van. We were being taken to a place called the Global Child Initiative.

We distracted the drivers so they crashed into a wall, then we quickly got out of the van and ran away. "They're following us," I said nervously.

"Quick, run into that tunnel," Michael murmured.

"I think we got away," Bob whispered.

"What should we do? We can't go back to our families or they might get us again," Kevin said, crying.

"We need to run!"

Matty Dolan (11)
The Wigston Academies Trust, Wigston

The Boy

Once you know something, you can't unknow it. I wish I didn't know things, things that I'm not supposed to know, things that could get us all in danger. Things that have got us in danger...

The sirens wailed painfully loud as the boy's torn hospital gown blew in the wind. We crouched behind a bush not far from the factory, gasping for breath. I tried to think back to my life before any of this but my senses were overwhelmed and my heart pounded heavily.

The boy turned to me with a sad smile, he knew it was over.

Raegan Erin Hamp (13)
The Wigston Academies Trust, Wigston

Beast Hunt

There was a trainer who was hunting for beasts called Pokémon. The trainer's name was Ash Ketchum and the Pokémon was called Mimikyu, the ghost and dark type, and Ash's Pokémon was called Pikachu.

As soon as the trainer approached the Pokémon, Pikachu used thunderbolt on Mimikyu but Mimikyu used shadow ball. So Ash told Pikachu to use iron tail and quick attack and it hit Mimikyu four times and got it weak.

So Ash threw a Poké Ball and caught Mimikyu and had a new member of the team.

Owen Lunn (11)
The Wigston Academies Trust, Wigston

Sirens!

The sirens wailed in the distance; I didn't move. They were searching for me! I'd escaped. Finally done it, broken out. Never going back! Fifteen long years in that prison - for a crime I didn't commit.

I had to make it to the other side of the city. Out of here for good! Creeping through the deserted alleyways, pausing every time the sirens approached. I was almost there. I could see her waiting for me. Ready to start our life together. I sprinted across the street and into the car. "Step on it!"

She did. We were on our way.

Paige Sherwin (13)
The Wigston Academies Trust, Wigston

The Chase

I was running so quickly, but I couldn't stop now. My legs ached, my body was bruised and hurt. They wouldn't stop running either.

It was getting dark; nowhere to hide, nowhere to sleep. On turned their torches, which lightened up the path behind me, but I kept on running. I was in the forest, birds and owls flew over me but nothing else to be heard or seen.

I'd finally lost them. The hunters were gone. I was safe at last. Out of breath, I slowly walked home. Every noise I heard made me jump. Was I actually safe?

Hannah Vann (13)
The Wigston Academies Trust, Wigston

The Alien Invasion

I had twenty-four hours to escape from the alien invasion.
"Oh no! They're coming!" The twenty-four hours had started.
I ran as fast as I could, that was a bad idea. I was breathless
but that didn't stop me. I carried on, I persevered, I never
gave up. Instead of running to my heart's content, I speed-
walked instead.
I ran past broken skyscrapers falling past broken UFOs. I
even jumped over a ditch. A UFO landed next to me. I had to
hide! I heard really loud breathing next to me.
Suddenly, I felt a hand on my shoulder.

Harry Wells (11)
The Wigston Academies Trust, Wigston

Watching The Hunted

They realised they weren't alone, that I had been watching their every move. Malisa was shaking whilst Walter was praying. I turned around and they were both searching for something, a weapon. I stood up and she killed me. It was the strangest feeling of my life, and the last feeling of my life. Malisa had a locket and inside there was a blade. She grabbed it and slashed it on my throat.

I tried to save myself, I never planned to hurt either of them, only a little bit of fun. However, it was the end. I'd been hunted.

Maisie Keane (13)
The Wigston Academies Trust, Wigston

Escape The Nightmare

I couldn't run for much longer. My heart raced and my blood was pumping. They weren't far behind but I was close, close to freedom.

Seven long years in this place and I'd had enough. I had to escape and this was my only chance. I turned a corner and there it was, the wall. All I had to do was climb this and then I would be free, free from this nightmare.

They were close, so close that I could hear their footsteps getting closer and closer; the sound echoing loudly. Then I jumped. I was over. I'd escaped.

Freya Mistry (13)
The Wigston Academies Trust, Wigston

The Mask

We locked eyes. All my progress... gone. I had to escape without being caught but it was impossible. It was like he'd put a tracking device on me. Had he?

I only had ten minutes to reach the light before the world got wiped out. I knew there was a vent behind me that I could escape through, but without him hearing? No.

I had to escape. I carefully placed my hands on the screws and rotated them as slowly as possible. I placed the screws on the ground, removed the vent from its place and escaped. Finally, my freedom.

Macauli Moran (13)
The Wigston Academies Trust, Wigston

Wanted

I had twenty-four hours to catch a criminal. The sirens were wailing. Now the prisoner knew we were coming.

It was dangerous. The criminal had been spotted, so we ran and ran but I couldn't run anymore. It was starting to get dark and we had lost him.

The west police group had found a dead body; the evidence had to be there somewhere. It was getting very late now, and I hadn't caught this criminal. The police force were relying on me. He was killing more each day.

It was time. I knew what I had to do.

Macey Jane Liquorish (13)
The Wigston Academies Trust, Wigston

The Police Chase

I heard the noise of the piercing siren. They were coming to get me. I looked around; nobody was close to me. Suddenly, the officers slammed the car door shut. They saw me.
I made a run for it. They were metres away from me. I dashed around a sharp bend. I came to a halt, I turned around. I had lost them so I casually started walking home, when something suspicious took place.
I heard a rustle coming from a nearby bush. Then two people popped out. The officers surrounded me. I couldn't escape. They took me away.

Ruby Kendall (11)
The Wigston Academies Trust, Wigston

The Hunter Becomes The Hunted

As I prowled along the muddy shoals of the river, my paws sank like quicksand. I was drawn nearer within the seconds to my destiny, which awaited me, almost ready to pounce in its path. Until the blinding light of the flashlights scarred my vision of what awaited. They grabbed me by the fur collar, ragging me like a football, as my ears pointed down to the snow-covered floor, in fright of what was to come. I heard the engine rumble as my heart started beating louder by the second. What was going to happen to me now?

Marissa Faye McFarlane (12)

The Wigston Academies Trust, Wigston

24 Hours

I had twenty-four hours to press the button without getting seen by the zombies. I was locked in my house, which was completely a mess, and all I could hear was the rustling noise of the trees blowing in the wind.

And now the time had come - I had to leave the house. I opened the old brown door and sprinted outside. I saw hideous zombies. The one that really caught my eye was a zombie with an eye perfectly in place and another eye hanging down by a thread.

I was so close to pressing the button, but...

Tia Hill (11)
The Wigston Academies Trust, Wigston

Hunted

I still have nightmares about it to this day. In the middle of a street, as midnight struck, I stood there, breathless. I looked behind myself and saw the colour of flaming-hot torches in the distance. I took off.

I ran as fast as my legs could carry me. Now, I must've been at least five hundred feet from where I'd started. I saw the crowd of people walking with fire. I bolted again until my legs could run no more.

I saw them but I was trapped. I then realised that I had become the hunted.

Jack Smart (12)
The Wigston Academies Trust, Wigston

Hunted

My legs burn, my throat's coarse, but still, I must run. I must run until I'm free. Free from them. Free from Capitil. Free from the devastating war.

I hear a droning noise, my head whips around. I'm facing a drone. It must be from Capitil, I think. I turn and run.

I suddenly stop as I hear a rustle. I notice a solider, hidden in the bushes. It is Commander Connix, I know it. I seize my knife. As quick as lightning, I plunge it deep into her heart. Then, *bang!* A gunshot. I am dead.

Woody Orton (13)
The Wigston Academies Trust, Wigston

The Creepy Old Lady

We had to leave...

One summer's day, I was out with my friends and it all went wrong. Sam (the popular boy) had crept into this old, abandoned house and it turned out an elderly woman owned it. She was shouting at us and Sam.

She then took out her phone and began to ring the police. We ran and ran and ran. We then came to this field and hid in the water. For the hour we had been in there, we heard multiple police cars drive past.

After we got out of the water, we worriedly sprinted home.

Lili Rutter (12)
The Wigston Academies Trust, Wigston

The Final Race

It was the last mile and the enemy was closing in. Branches, stones and mud flying up after every step. There was a mile to go, and John decided to dig deep and pelt on. Paint bullets coming from every angle, it was John and his enemy left. He wanted to be the only one at the finish line, so he cut a corner. The enemy continued on straight. Running as fast as he could, John managed to get to ten metres before the finish line and hid behind a bush.

The enemy was close, John took his final shot...

Frances Mitchell (12)

The Wigston Academies Trust, Wigston

Betrayal

I couldn't run for much longer, the wasteland stretched out further than I could imagine. It was just me and my friend, running from... him.
Where would we go next? It was a clear path as far as the eye could see, with no place to hide. Suddenly, she started to slow down; I thought about continuing but I couldn't.
Little did I know that she would be the one to run from.
All of a sudden, she was the one pointing a weapon at me.
Why would she do this? From then, I knew it was the end.

Milly Jade Shaw (12)
The Wigston Academies Trust, Wigston

Chase!

I had twenty-four hours. I was an escaped convict on my way to a remote village. All I wanted was to get out. To live a better life. I didn't want to be in a prison cell for my whole life, for a crime I didn't commit.

The police were hot on my tail. My lungs were giving out; I felt like I was going to faint. All I kept telling myself was, you're so close, just a bit longer.

I needed time. Time to build a new life, time to explain, just time. But suddenly... *Bang! Bang!*

Sara Filali (12)
The Wigston Academies Trust, Wigston

24 Hours

I had twenty-four hours. The shivers that were in my leg were now near my spine. It was a bleak, dark night and, for the first time, I was alone. But I wanted to be because danger was near. A man wanted to use my powers.
It wasn't safe. They knew who I was and that my powers were beyond this world. The night got colder, I knew that I had to get to sleep but I knew that they'd find me. I hadn't slept for a week so it was time to take a nap.
Suddenly, footsteps awoke me.

Grace Sheffield (11)

The Wigston Academies Trust, Wigston

Hunted

I still have nightmares about it. It was summer and I was taking a quiet stroll through the woods. I heard a loud gunshot behind me and when I looked back... the gun was aiming at me.

I spared no time and I bolted it. It felt like I had been running for hours. Breathlessly, I screamed, "Why are you doing this to me?" I was trembling with fear and I wanted to collapse but I didn't.

Alas, I was no match, I was struck down. And with my last breath, I said, "I love you, mum."

Eleanor Reece-Sumner (12)

The Wigston Academies Trust, Wigston

The Chase

I could hear it, it was sprinting. All I had to do was get to the station. Once I was there it would be fine. I could see it in the distance and I could hear it. Corpses all around, the thing must have outrun them. The setting around me was a wood, too dark to see very far in front of me. But suddenly, in the distance, I saw the station.

Eventually, I got there, slammed the door and escaped onto the train. When I looked out of the window, I could see it. Never ever again.

Louis Cockshaw (12)

The Wigston Academies Trust, Wigston

Confused

How did I get myself into this mess? My head was spinning with thoughts as I ran through the dreary woods. Why did I do it? Because I trusted him. I didn't want to do it. In my head, I didn't. But the blood on my hands told me a different story...

I had until midnight. I had two minutes. All I needed to do was pull the trigger. The fear in her eyes, I didn't want to do it. But I did. *Bang!*

She fell to the floor. I wanted to go to her but I ran.

Emma-Louise Little (12)
The Wigston Academies Trust, Wigston

Sweet Revenge

Finally, after so many years, I found him. He was in his hideout. I moved to a vantage point and took out all his men. It was a bloodbath.

I moved in. I saw him. He ran but I was close behind. We both took cover. He was behind the boxes so long, I thought he'd ran. He hit me on the back of my head, he hit me to the ground, but I stabbed him in the leg.

"This is revenge," I said. I shot him in the stomach and watched his insides spew out. And I left.

Martin John Bourne-Fisher (12)

The Wigston Academies Trust, Wigston

Escape Room!

Twenty-four hours to get out of this room. Someone was trying to kill me.

I was trapped in some kind of cage. There was a box beside me with a clue inside. I opened the box and the clue said, 'I am something that you can use when you don't have keys'. I thought and thought, then it clicked. It was a pin to pick the lock. So I grabbed one out of my hair and forced it in. They said it was hard but I got out. There was a man behind me, he had a knife.

Isobel Henderson (11)
The Wigston Academies Trust, Wigston

Forest Hunt

"We have to leave, now!" Nova glanced at her friend, Lightning.

He picked his longbow up and nodded. They both knew it was too dangerous to stay in the forest.

Nova grabbed her axe as she heard a branch snap. "They found us, run!" she yelled.

Lightning looked over his shoulder as he heard their pursuers panting. They ran faster, as they could hear their claws scratching the dried leaves on the forest floor.

Nova gasped as she realised they had been surrounded. Lightning heard a piercing howl. Glowing red eyes stared through the dark forest. Suddenly, everything went black.

Morgan Ellen Armer (14)

Wellfield High School, Leyland

Hunted

It was a foggy night, the twilight moon shone through the leaves of the eerie trees that lined the thicket on the outskirts of the town. Behind the gentle breath of the wind, the cocking of the rifle disturbed the silence.

The barrel pointed at a cold-hearted, human-shaped silhouette that suddenly stopped, observed the surroundings, only to start running again. Faster than any human being, looking for an unlucky victim to attack.

Calm breaths came from the vengeful slayer. Controlling his anger, he lined up the shot as if he knew the future. He pulled the trigger without hesitation... *bang!*

Leon Whatton (15)
Wellfield High School, Leyland

Whatever A Clock Stands For

The sound is suffocating, piercing, intoxicating. Ruling over us, dictating each move made. Gnawing at our feet, picking at our brains - making sure that once it pounces we're weak enough to succumb.

It gets bored, sometimes. Strikes early - plays games with the victim and watches as the dominoes fall - entire families fall. It laughs in glee as it continues. Doesn't stop for anything, anyone. Claws through our skin, eats at our hearts with its merciless, cruel, taunting nature. It's everywhere. *Tick-tock. Tick-tock.* Rushing you and pulling you in. Time hunts me down.

Ellie D
Wellfield High School, Leyland

The Strange Figure

As the sky got darker, the scarier and more dangerous it got. Many people rushed into their homes before sunset as there were rumours of a strange figure that wandered around the town at night...

Of course, not everyone believed what the rumours said. One night, a young man decided to see the strange figure that everyone was talking about. As he wandered quietly, he heard footsteps following him.

He turned around but there was nothing there. Fear started to build up. Before he could escape and go home, everything went black. He fell onto the ground with bloodstains everywhere.

Pearl Xu (14)

Wellfield High School, Leyland

The Doll

I was sat in the cramped closet. We were playing hide-and-seek in the old hill-house. Fingernail-like taps were hitting the door handle, shaking the door.

"What the-?" I got up. It stopped.

My hand shakily reached for the handle. Grabbing it, slowly pushing the door open. Silence crept on me. I looked around the room, I saw it. Sat there, its eyes stared right at me, piercing my body like daggers. The doll.

She was porcelain with her pink ruffle-dress and blonde curled hair and bright blue eyes that followed me around the room. Angelica was her name.

Maddy O'Neill
Wellfield High School, Leyland

Goodbye

"Beware of the serial kill..." *Zzz. Pop!* The TV lost signal. I knew going to the cabin in October would be a disaster! I could hear the animals walking outside, or maybe it was the killer... No, I couldn't let myself think like that. I spun around to face the window. A black figure stands facing me with bloodthirsty eyes. I blinked. It was gone. I went to sit down in my favourite chair when I heard creaking from my door. Footsteps were getting closer! Suddenly I felt a hot breath against my ear and heard a man whispering goodbye...

Abby Bamford (12)
Wellfield High School, Leyland

He Caught Me

I couldn't run much longer, my heart was beating a mile an hour. My lungs barely had any air, gasping at any air that I let in.

My arms were aching from him grabbing me, my elbow bleeding from falling after wriggling free. My head was bleeding after him punching me to knock me unconscious. I hid down a flooded alley in a bin, hoping that maybe, just maybe, he wouldn't find me. He came down the alley, shouting, "You can't hide from me, darlin'. I got you stuck." He lifted up every bin until mine - he caught me!

Bethany Moulding (13)
Wellfield High School, Leyland

Hunted

I still have nightmares about it. That night I mean. The air was thick and eerie. The uneasy feeling in my stomach began to grow. I felt like I was being watched, like everyone knew what I was planning. Everyone but me. My pace quickened. My heart began to pound. *Boom! Boom!* Like little fireworks in my ears gradually getting louder until, *bang!* I was scared. I was petrified. I began to run, adrenaline pumping all around my body. A siren wailed in the distance. "Oh no, they're here!"
A man appeared, one I knew all too well...

Amy Smith (12)
Wellfield High School, Leyland

Hunted

Running through the yellow, overgrown field, I ran away from the ear-piercing siren. Looking behind me, I could see him loading his gun and getting ready to aim for me. Frantically rooting through my dirty, ripped backpack I searched for my only chance of survival: my bow and arrow. I'd seen this happen to other people before but never in my life did I think this would happen to me.

The government had sent the best assassin in our city to kill me just because I knew things, things I shouldn't have known. I was being hunted...

Maddie Wilson-Burgess
Wellfield High School, Leyland

The Chase

I couldn't run for much longer, they were on my tail. They had large, black dogs chasing me down, metres away. I darted around every corner I could make out in the pitch-black darkness but they followed me everywhere.
I couldn't see anything in front of me so I tripped over anything in my path, allowing those fiends to catch up. My face was dripping with sweat. Running frantically, I dashed into the nearest block of flats. I bolted up thousands of steep stairs but sadly slipped dramatically.
The hunt was over. They got me.

Iain Weatherby (14)
Wellfield High School, Leyland

The Chase

Running through the green, dense forest, running from death. *Bang!* The killing machine gets fired and it makes all of the birds fly out of the treetops, out of their homes. While running, I come across a river and the killing machine is right behind me. I have to jump across to save myself and get back to my family and friends. So I jump over the river, he follows swiftly behind, shooting a bullet every five seconds.

I was being chased for at least thirty minutes before I managed to find a place to hide. *Bang!*

J Hynd (13)
Wellfield High School, Leyland

Breathe

Five, breathe in. Four, breathe out. Three, keep counting. Two, you're okay. One, just run.

My legs crumbled under my weight. I wasn't sure how much longer I could pace myself. I could hear him. His twisted laugh carried through the trees. His cold body wandering after me.

Every now and then a branch would snap, a bird would cry. Every time, my hair jolted up and it spurred me to run faster. I thought I was safe. I thought it was over. His shivering hands latched around my neck, paralyzing me. I let out a breath. It was over.

Shanice W
Wellfield High School, Leyland

Acceptance

It's not safe now; they know where we are. There's no way of survival, all we can do is run to our deaths.

If we look him in the eye, we're gone instantly. The Spaner twins went first, they had to watch each other die gruesome, gory deaths. Walking around the maze, if you even look up you're at risk of a horribly painful death.

I shouldn't be here. I had a family and now I'll never see them. I can hear those demons in the distance, slowing moving towards me. All I can do is accept my death here.

Hana Toulson (14)
Wellfield High School, Leyland

Moonlight

A small cabin in the dark forest briefly lit up, a rustle from the bush behind scared me. Then my leg was yanked... Red, glowing eyes stared into my eyes. The smell of burnt flesh filled my nose. I crawled back, hoping to free myself. A giant wolf walked out of the deep, green brush. It growled, blood dripping from its black lips. I finally got myself free. I ran but I was not faster. I heard twigs snapping, the black wolf ran beside me and leapt for me. It bit my neck; my sight went blurry. Darkness.

Kane Hampson (14)
Wellfield High School, Leyland

Over The Top

We were close. *One more year,* they thought. Six months at best.

Mud squelched behind us as we saw dead bodies scattered on the horizon. We were on the first line now. Over the top, he said. Whistles were blowing. It was a dooming effect. Men falling down everywhere, only two got to the other side. Me and Lewis, we had no idea what we were doing. Bullets flew everywhere.

Silence. The world went cold. Blood dripped down to the muddy trench floor. I was just another scattered body with no identity.

Dawn Dyson (13)
Wellfield High School, Leyland

The Criminal Who Killed My Family

I still have nightmares about it. The time they took away my family and tortured them right in front of me. The dread of them hurting me is a massive fear...

The man dragged me out of the metal cage aggressively and tried hurting me. I ran fast, out of the room, and called the police. The man was chasing me with a gun.

I finally reached the cloudy, miserable outside and was banging on every door, trying to get help, but nobody answered. I wandered slowly to a petrol station and waited for the police to turn up.

Molly McSweeney (14)
Wellfield High School, Leyland

Zombies

I had twenty-four hours to get away. I looked out of my window and all I could see were people running, dead bodies, and flashing lights everywhere. My hearing was deafened by the sirens and screaming from outside. *Crash!* It came from my door. I ran to the kitchen to grab a knife.

I made my way slowly towards the door, as I saw it had fallen and zombies were out there. Although I was scared, I knew I had to face the challenge I was given. I crept outside and they heard me. I immediately knew I was doomed.

Elise Jennifer Erin Hustings (13)
Wellfield High School, Leyland

Surrounded And Betrayed

Were they here? It is hard to tell, reality had been a blur and yet could I really call it that? Everything I knew was just a projection. Why, why did they hurt me? How could they cause this pain? Everything is pursuing me! Mindless beings after me, taking my form, my will. I dread what will happen if they find me. They can track me, nowhere is unbeknownst to them! I must quieten. How they tap truly terrifies me, scraping their way in. If anyone is out there, please help! I don't want this, I beg of you...

Ashley Jones (13)
Wellfield High School, Leyland

The Quest Of Time

I had eight hours to complete my quest to find and capture the murderer. His codename was Ronaldo. He had committed more crimes by kicking many footballs at people's windows and smashing them! He didn't replace them or give any money. I had to get on a plane and catch him. I had to get to the airport. I only had four hours left! Then I saw him. I pulled him out of his seat and chucked him out of the plane! He luckily grabbed onto the top of the plane! He was annoyed. I joined him. This was war!

Zack James Bingham (12)

Wellfield High School, Leyland

The Chase

It was coming. Death was around the corner. I was still running, without a clue what could happen. Coming to a stop, I gazed at the view ahead... I soon realised my mistake. The sirens were wailing and as I turned around I was blinded by flashlights. I started running again, as fast as my legs could take me.

The sirens got louder and louder and I knew I'd been spotted. It was close.

Eventually, I came to a wall, a dead-end. I stopped, put my back against it, I had no hope. It was over...

Kieran T
Wellfield High School, Leyland

Police Chase

The sirens wailed. The citizens ran. I grabbed the money and fled in the car. My mates got in the back and we were off at the speed of light.

We tried to go uptown to try and find somewhere safe but it only got worse, there were more police cars, more helicopters and more sounds of gunshots. I swiftly drifted the car the other way to turn south, however, it just got even worse somehow. I didn't know what to do. Then we went over some police spikes and I heard shot after shot. Everyone was dead.

Jude Chambers (12)
Wellfield High School, Leyland

Being Watched

One night, in December, I was walking home from my school which is around 25-minute walk. I felt like something was wrong so I decided to go the long way which is around 10 more minutes.

I get to this really open street and I see a man dressed in black with his head down. I started to speed up. Not far from my house, the guy was still close so I decided to run home.

I made it home and locked the door. Not long after, someone was knocking at my door. I heard a crack, the door opened...

Seth Wright
Wellfield High School, Leyland

The Monsters

I felt like I was being watched. I definitely felt this before. It was strange. I felt someone behind me! I spun around, confused. It was the thing I feared the most. It was the monster I'd run from for years! I ran as fast as I could. It followed me. I tried not to make noise. If you made noise, it would hear you. They are faster than you think! I ran into a man. He looked like he was going to scream. I got away from him as he screamed. I saw it! The long, tall, freaky creator...

Ashleigh Tinsley
Wellfield High School, Leyland

It Waits...

I must stay concealed, I cannot move a muscle. It is there, waiting for me. The room reeks of decay and death. My accomplices' corpses litter the cold floor! We were caught at the wrong time at the wrong place. I checked beforehand and there is only one exit, where right now, it is waiting for me. I admit to doing wrong in my past. I admit I felt it was required. We got what we deserved and have been discovered! Should any man genuinely die this way? It is too late! The door opens...

Thomas Oxley (12)
Wellfield High School, Leyland

The Big Escape

It is November thirteenth 2024 and I'm locked in my cell. I have a plan. A plan I've had for years. If anyone can pull it off, it's me. I'm in the local state county jail, Cell B. In my cell there's an air vent behind my bed. The screws are a bit loose. I've made a makeshift screwdriver from a fork from the canteen, supplied by my friend Jerome. I've got a guard's uniform which Jerome got me as well. Don't ask how he got it. Anyway, I think I'm ready. It's time for the big escape...

Arran Gray (13)
Wellfield High School, Leyland

Lockdown

The ten-second bell started, which was the sign of a lockdown. I was stuck in the corridor, trying to get into the locked classrooms.

Scrambling down the corridor, I tried to find a classroom to get into but failed. I found an unlocked door but it was a small room full of cleaning equipment. I had to squeeze in underneath a shelf that was half as tall as me.

My heart was racing. Then, I heard another ten-second bell, meaning the end of the lockdown. I sighed in relief.

Reece Bowling (13)
Wellfield High School, Leyland

Nightmares

It was about three years ago when I almost lost my life. The nightmare of it still haunts me to this day.

I thought it was just a regular morning but was I wrong! I got up out of bed and got ready for work and went out to catch the bus. But the bus never arrived. I waited and waited, it was 9:00am and I was already late.

Boom! The rotting whiff of corpses hit me in the face. People started to run. I jumped in a dustbin and waited for the creature to return.

Maddison Parfitt
Wellfield High School, Leyland

The Hunt Of The Yard

One cold morning in a scrapyard I couldn't run for much longer. The sirens wailed. I was enclosed. They knew that I was there! The only way out was to fight. It was not safe. I could also climb but if I fell, I would die! I had twenty-four hours left to live... They were quickly containing the area, I needed to act now before they caught me! I tried to flee. They spotted me. They were pursuing me quicker than before! Out of breath, I wasn't being caught today...

Mason Gardner (13)
Wellfield High School, Leyland

Hunted

Hunted. Chased out of our homes. Footsteps neared and sirens wailed.

They were running blindly - slaughtered in front of my eyes. They were dying... for nothing. It was my pack's turn. The sirens stopped - we went in. We were the hunted. Blood all over. Hunted. Gone.

My fur was pressing against my back as I ran in front of my pack. They were picked off one by one. Soon it was only me - I knew it wouldn't last much longer. The humans were catching up.

Maddison R
Wellfield High School, Leyland

Hot Pursuit

I had twenty-four hours to do a job, if not I would be hunted down and killed. As I couldn't complete the job, I got into a hot pursuit! In order to escape, I had to jump over cars, climb on roofs and jump off cranes as I slipped through a tiny window. I looked behind me and saw the man chasing me! I ran straight through the wall and he chased me until I could not go much further. I carried on until he could not see me anymore! I hid away...

Matthew Meadows (12)
Wellfield High School, Leyland

The Bloody Hand!

It is real. It is all true. It was I that killed the girl that night. It was I that ripped her soul out of her chest. It was I, Jack the Ripper! The bloody hands are mine. It was a Saturday night. All was quiet and that was when I pounced on my next victim. I tiptoed quietly and opened the door, and then I pounced! I grabbed the knife and went for the kill! The job was done. I reached into her body and ripped her heart out! I ran out and left...

Amelia Finch (12)
Wellfield High School, Leyland

Zombies

It's not safe now they know where I am... I must hide like a chameleon in the shadows.
"Brains!"
Oh, shoot! I saw them coming so I ran across the building and I attacked and ran from the horde. I had an AK-47 in my hands and I fought for about twenty minutes. I ran out so I got my katana and I killed all the zombies! I ran to a safehouse. Then I saw another horde! I fought and fought and won!

Toms Trahovcevs
Wellfield High School, Leyland

Hide

We have to leave. Now! I don't know where they are but they are going to be here soon, they will hurt us. Quick, hide - they're here... we need to hide before they hurt us.
Hiding in the garage, we realise the door opens from the inside. Just in time, we get in the car and drive off. They must have heard us - they're running for their car. Following close behind us, I have to push my foot down to make our getaway.

Keira H (14)
Wellfield High School, Leyland

24 Hours

I had twenty-four hours to find the murderer. He had a blue banana on his arm but he was on his way to LA and I had to get him ASAP! I got in my Lamborghini Aventador SPL500. I acted quickly and I was on my way to LA! I knew I was going to get badly hurt so I got my hunting started! I was in my gorgeous Lambo and I was on his tail. I drifted around buildings, climbing up and down cars, buildings and much more... Then I got him!

Ben Harwood (12)
Wellfield High School, Leyland

YoungWriters® Est. 1991

YOUNG WRITERS INFORMATION

We hope you have enjoyed reading this book – and that you will continue to in the coming years.

If you're a young writer who enjoys reading and creative writing, or the parent of an enthusiastic poet or story writer, do visit our website **www.youngwriters.co.uk**. Here you will find free competitions, workshops and games, as well as recommended reads, a poetry glossary and our blog. There's lots to keep budding writers motivated to write!

If you would like to order further copies of this book, or any of our other titles, then please give us a call or order via your online account.

Young Writers
Remus House
Coltsfoot Drive
Peterborough
PE2 9BF
(01733) 890066
info@youngwriters.co.uk

Join in the conversation!
Tips, news, giveaways and much more!

f YoungWritersUK   **🐦** @YoungWritersCW